The Adventures
of
Sebastian Stone
and Violet

Copyright

Copyright 2024. Charisse Nechelle Bradley. All rights reserved.

No part of this publication may be reproduced, stored in a retrieval system, or transmitted, in any form or by any means, electronic or mechanical, including photocopy or recording, without the prior permission in writing of the publisher and the author, nor be otherwise circulated in any form of binding or cover than that in which it is published and without a similar condition including this condition being imposed on the subsequent purchaser. Thank you for your support of the author's rights.

This is a work of fiction. Names, characters, places, and incidents are either the products of the author's imagination or are used fictitiously. Any resemblance to actual persons, living or dead, events, or locales is entirely coincidental.

Dedication

This book is dedicated to the two most important people in my life, my mother and grandmother, who inspire me to keep going and continue pushing for what I want. As a child, I always had a wild imagination and often daydreamed in class. I have been writing for over twenty years. The idea for Sebastian Stone has been in the making for over ten years, and I'm finally glad I was able to bring it to fruition. The idea was a pitch for a movie, but it didn't pan out. So I turned it into a book, and here we are fourteen years later.

About The Author

Charisse holds a Master's degree in information science and is currently working in the field of information technology.

About The Book

What inspired me to write the book is to spread love, empower friendships, and acknowledge it's okay to be different and dream.

Quote by Charisse Nechelle Bradley

It's all right to be unique
Different is special
Dare, dream, and adventures
are at your fingertips!!

It's morning, and Brenda is in the kitchen making breakfast.

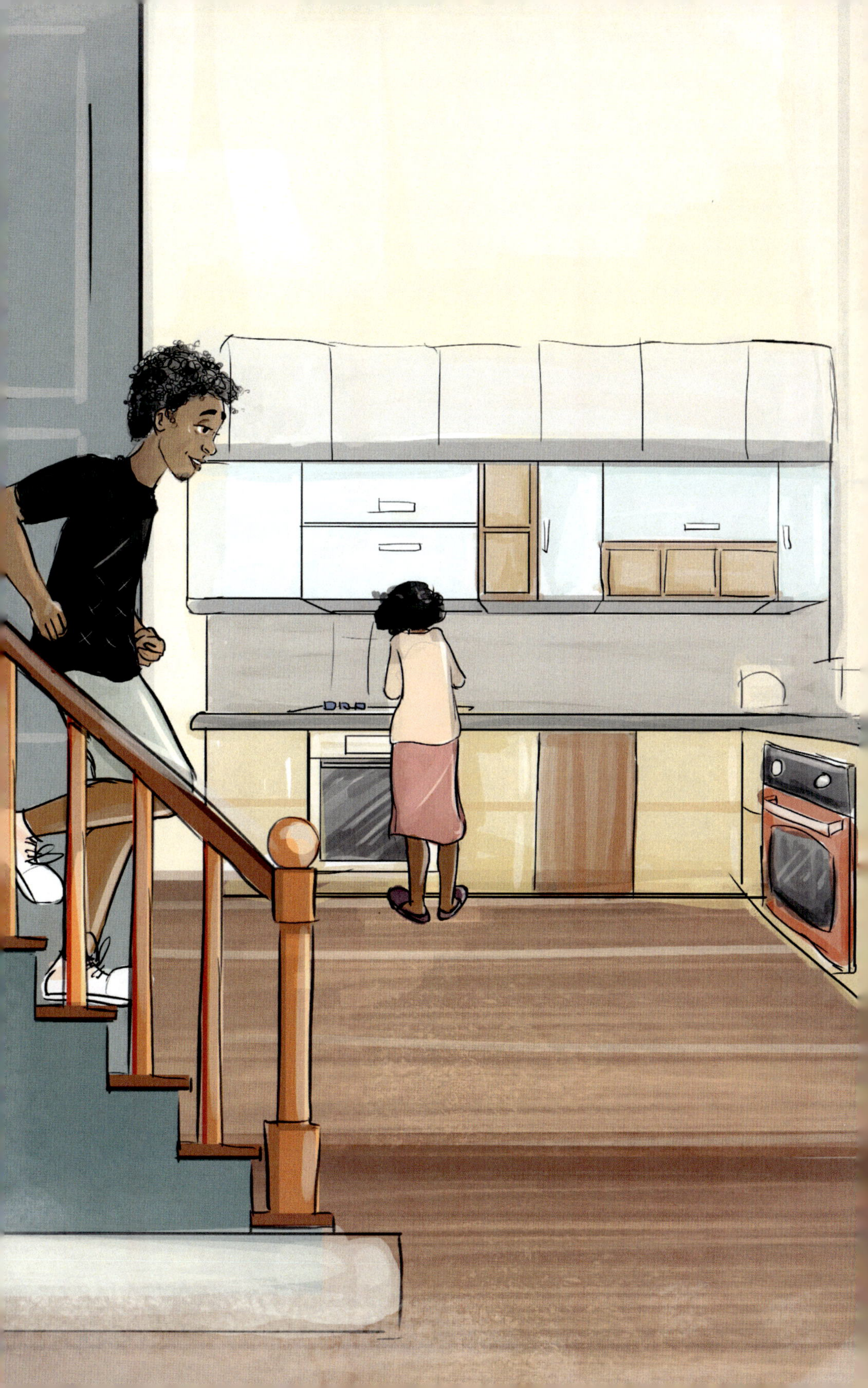

Brenda's phone rings. It's her husband, Robert, who is traveling on a work assignment. He is an archeologist, and he and his team have been in Egypt for months.

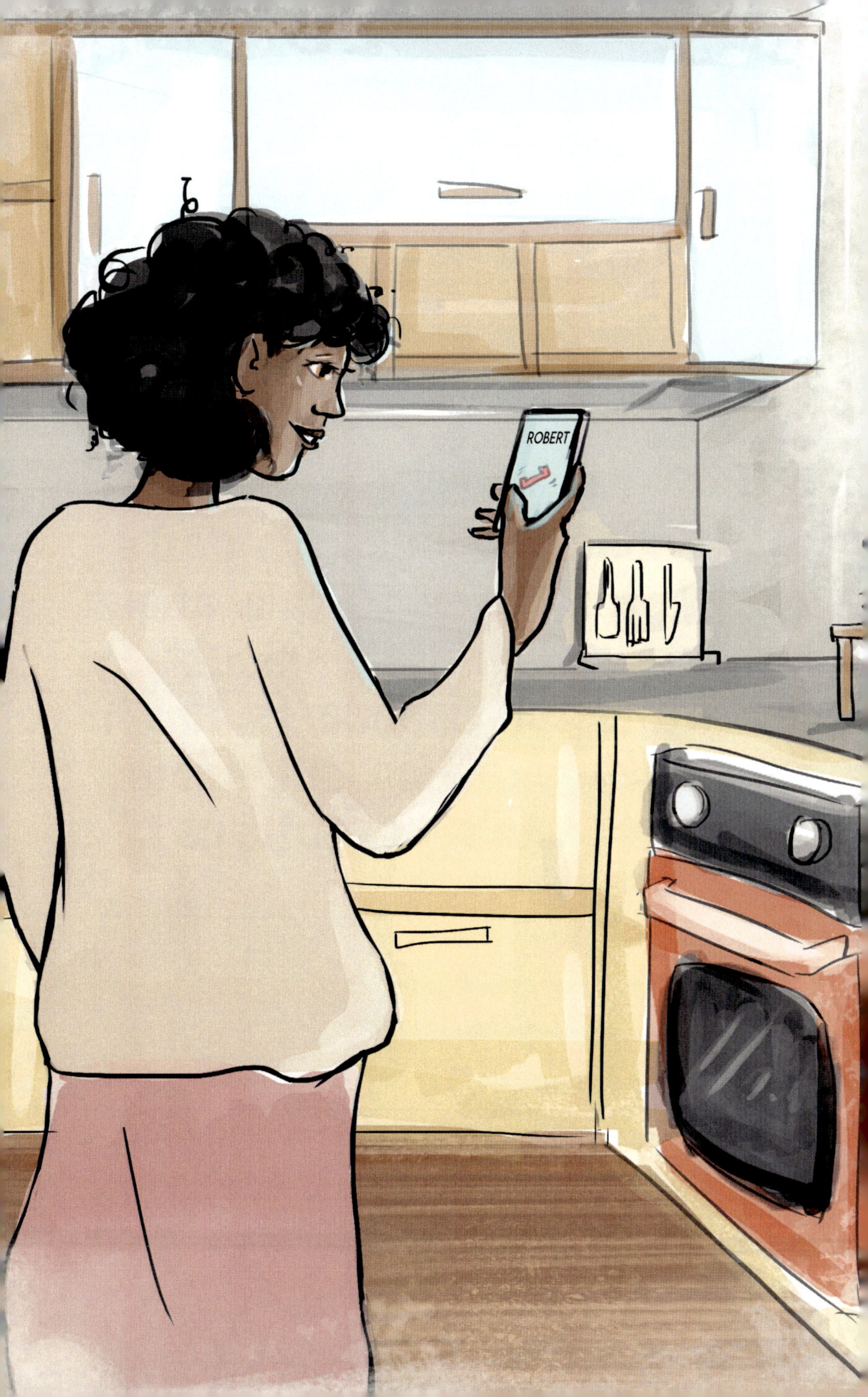
ROBERT

Sebastian loves his dad's job and loves to talk about his work. He anxiously waits for Brenda to finish talking to find out about his dad's adventures.

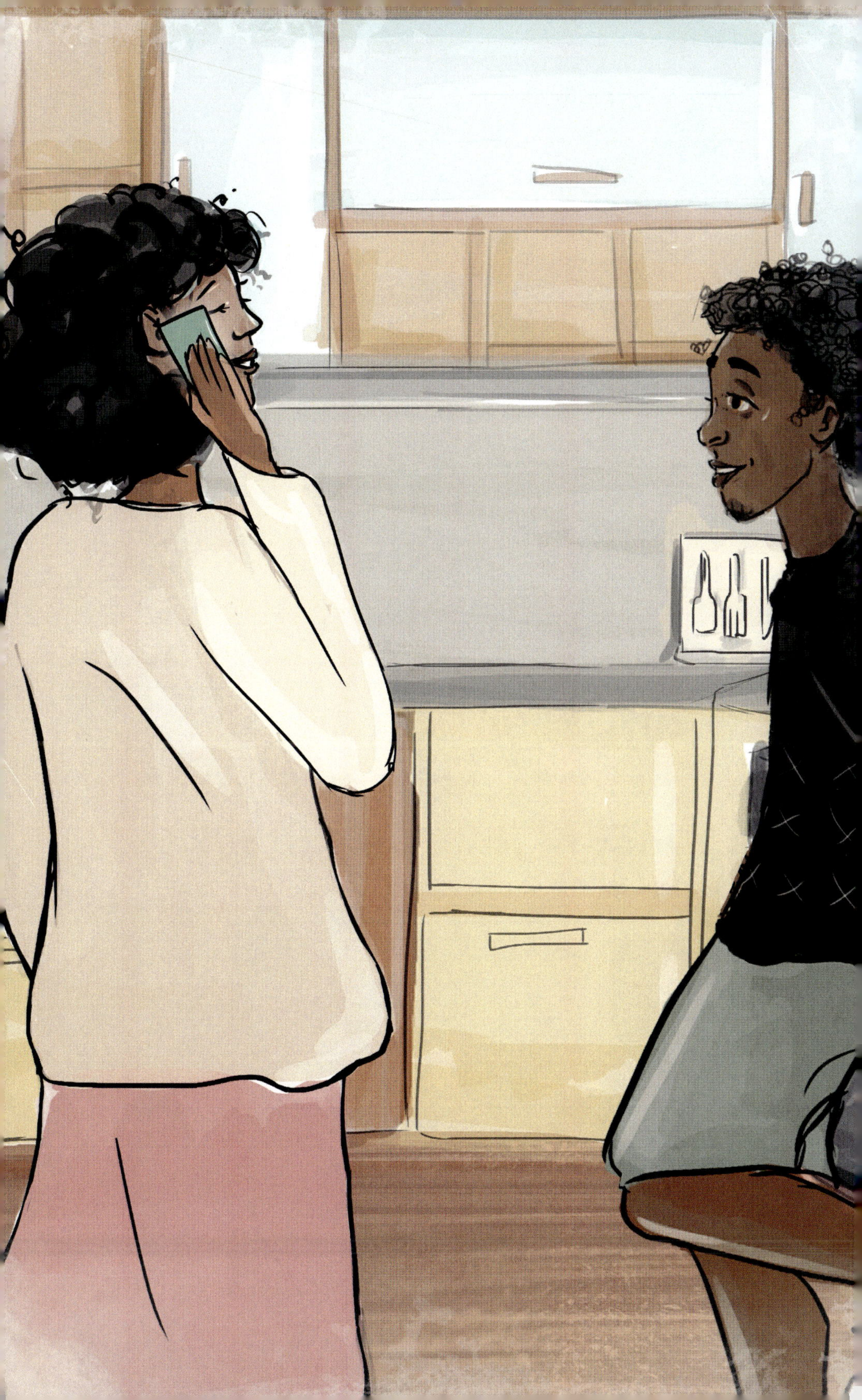

Sebastian lights up once he receives the phone. "Sebastian, how is my big guy, soon to be fifteen?" Hearing his dad's voice makes Sebastian smile.

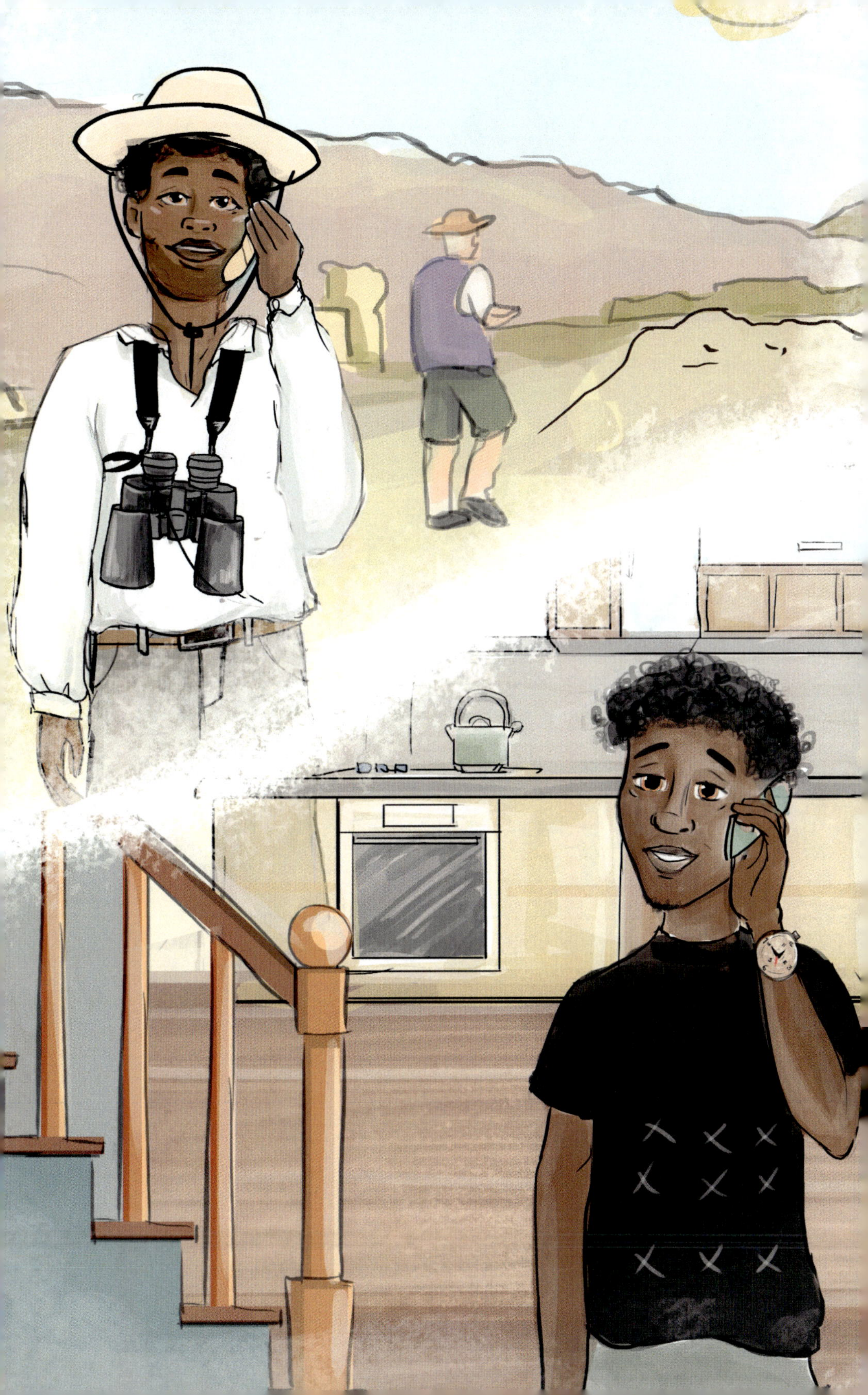

Robert says, "Well, I have something special for you." The doorbell rings. Brenda answers, and it's a package from Sebastian's dad.

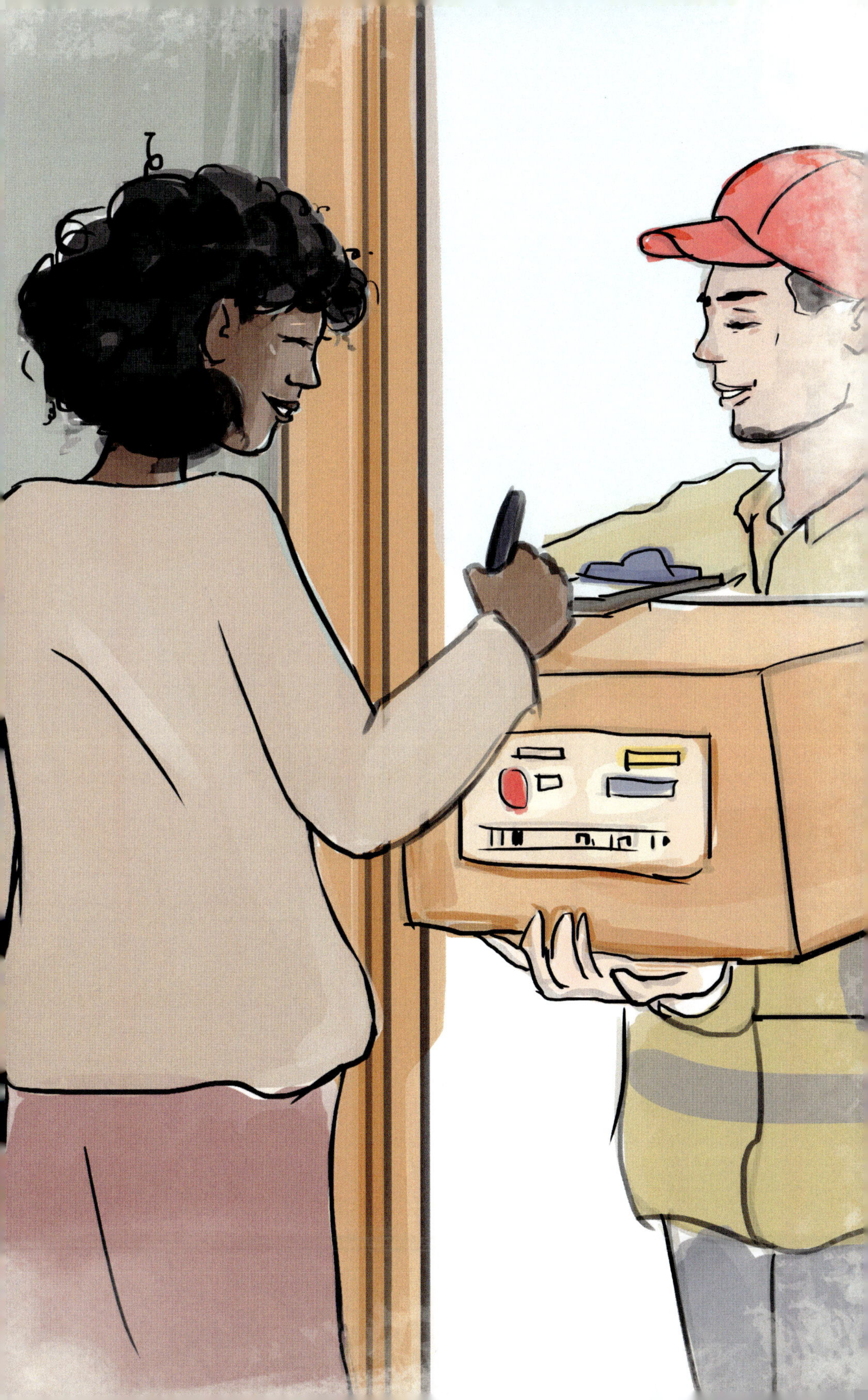

"Sebastian, it's for you."
Sebastian drops the
phone with excitement.

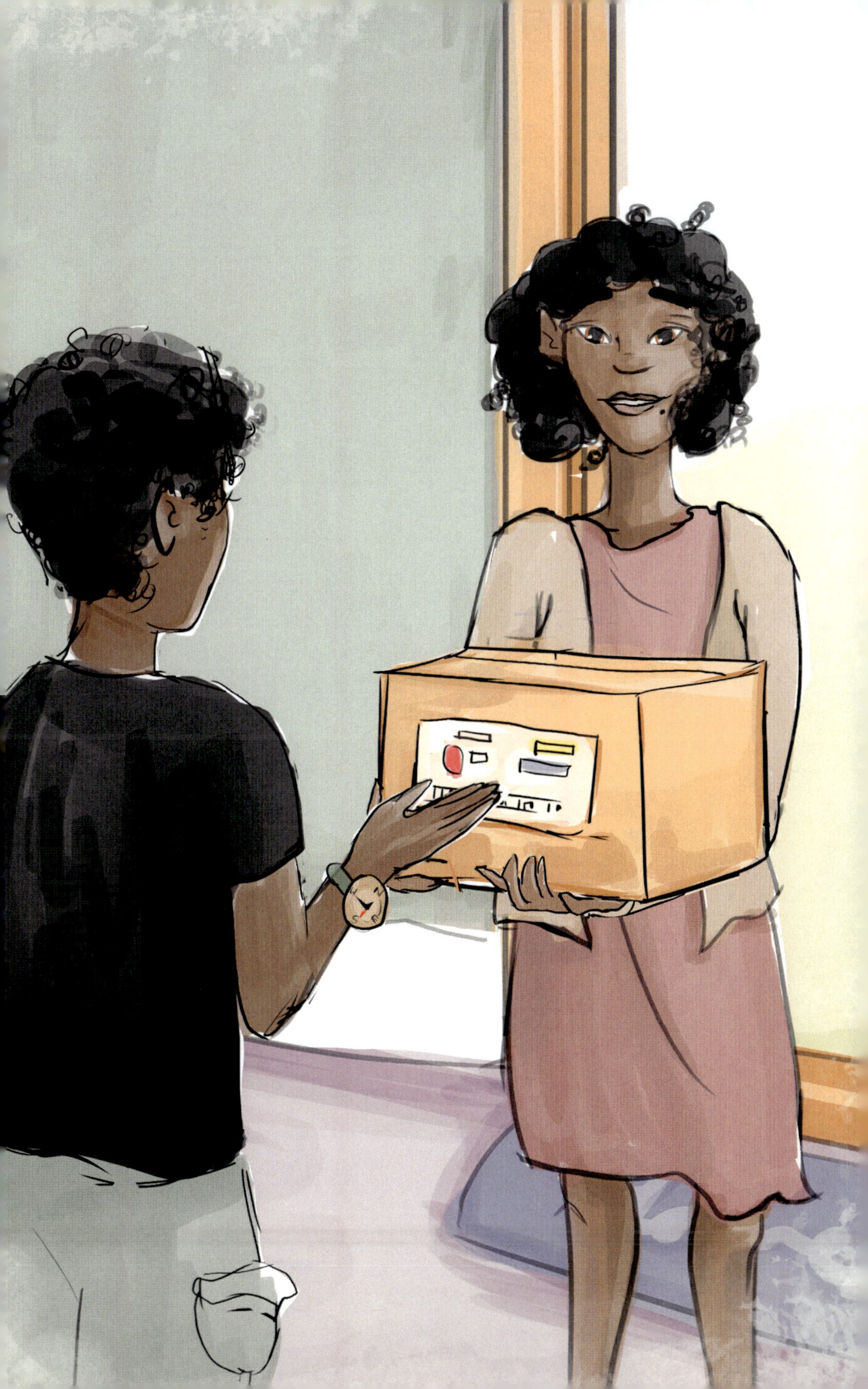

His mom smiles.
She picks up the phone,
"Greatest dad ever."

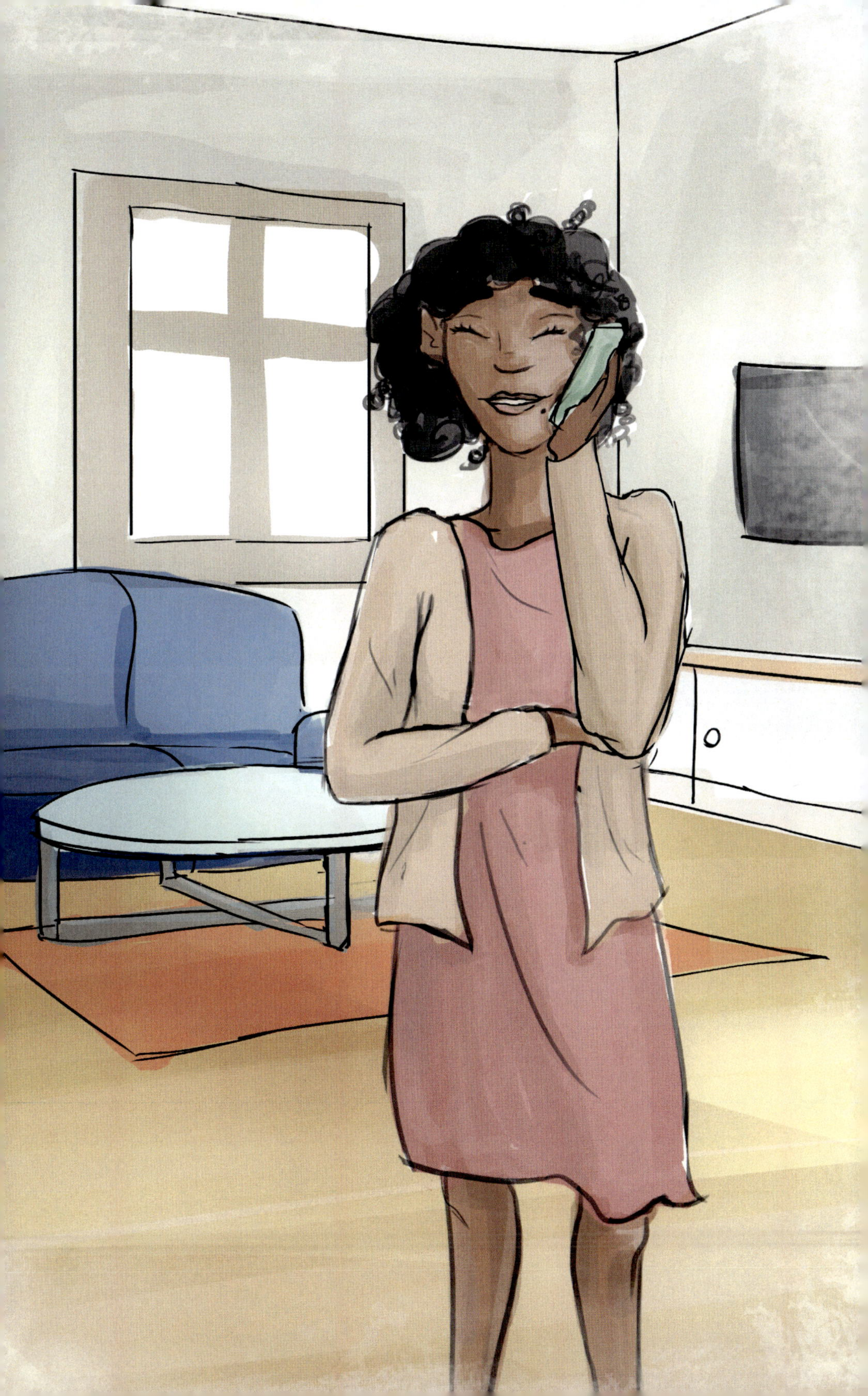

Sebastian opens his package and picks up the stones from inside the box, and he is clueless. Brenda hands the phone back to Sebastian.

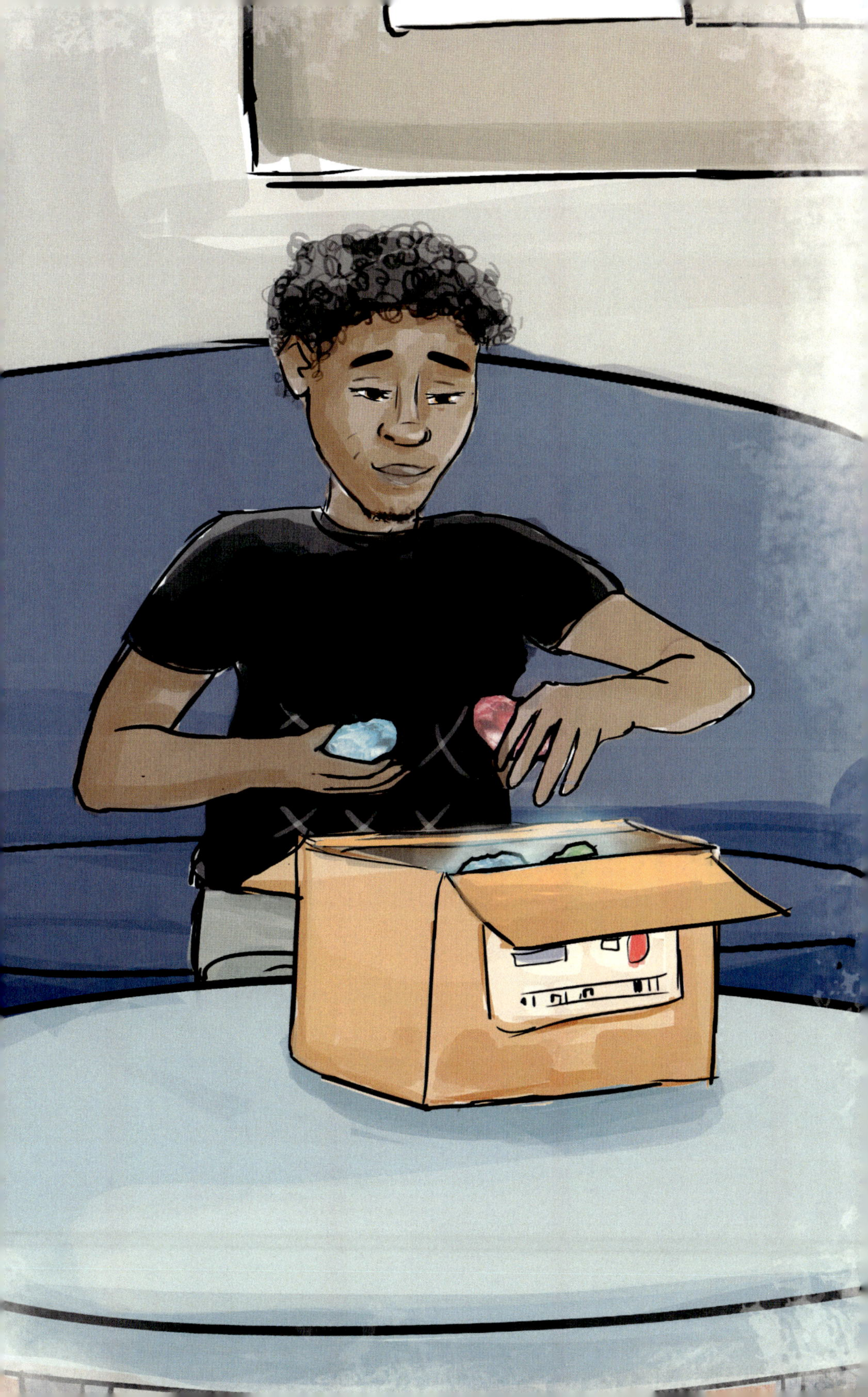

Dad says, "I hope you enjoy them they are special." Sebastian says, "What are they?

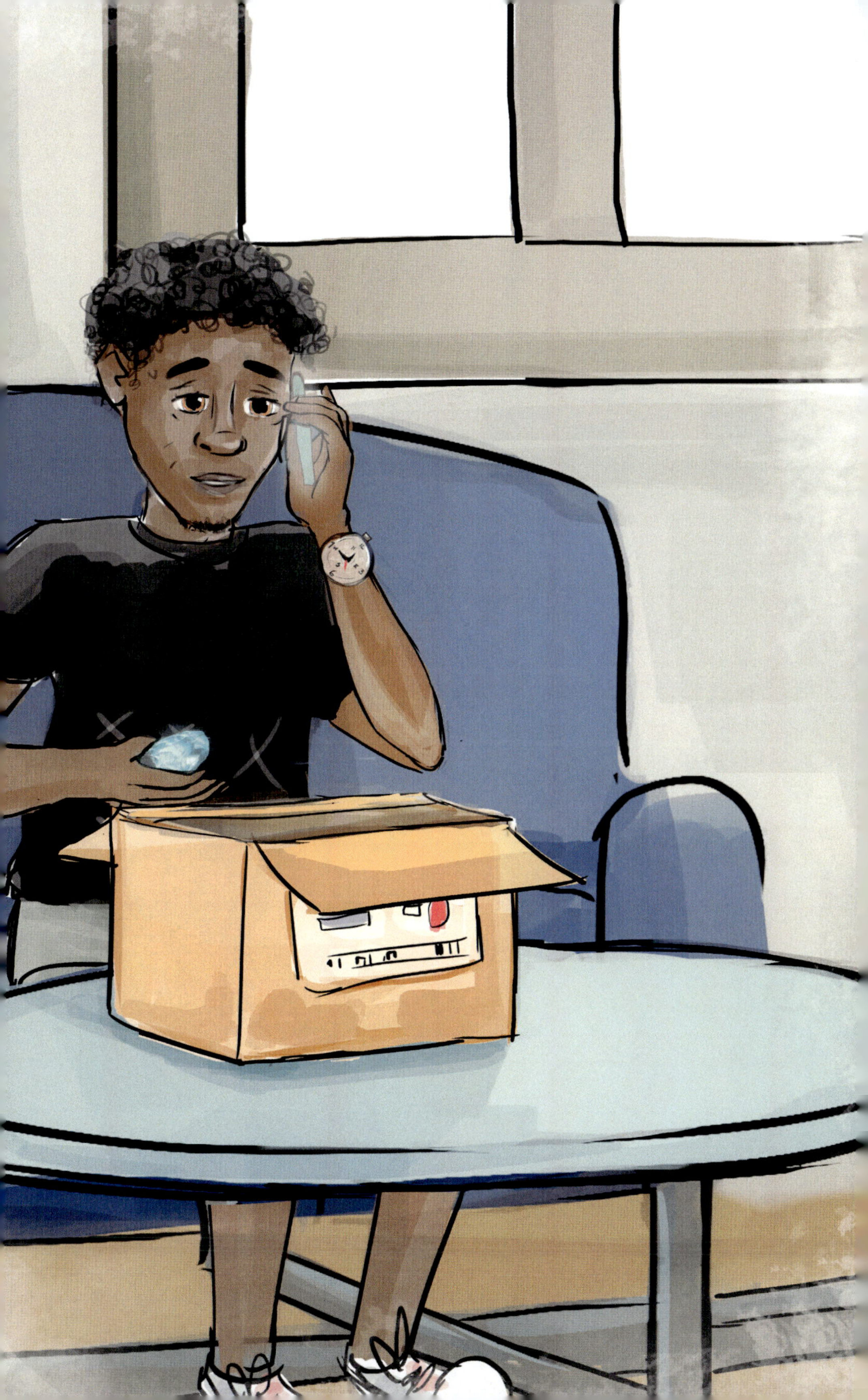

Dad says, "Trust me, son, they are special, just like you." Sebastian hangs up and heads to his bedroom with the package.

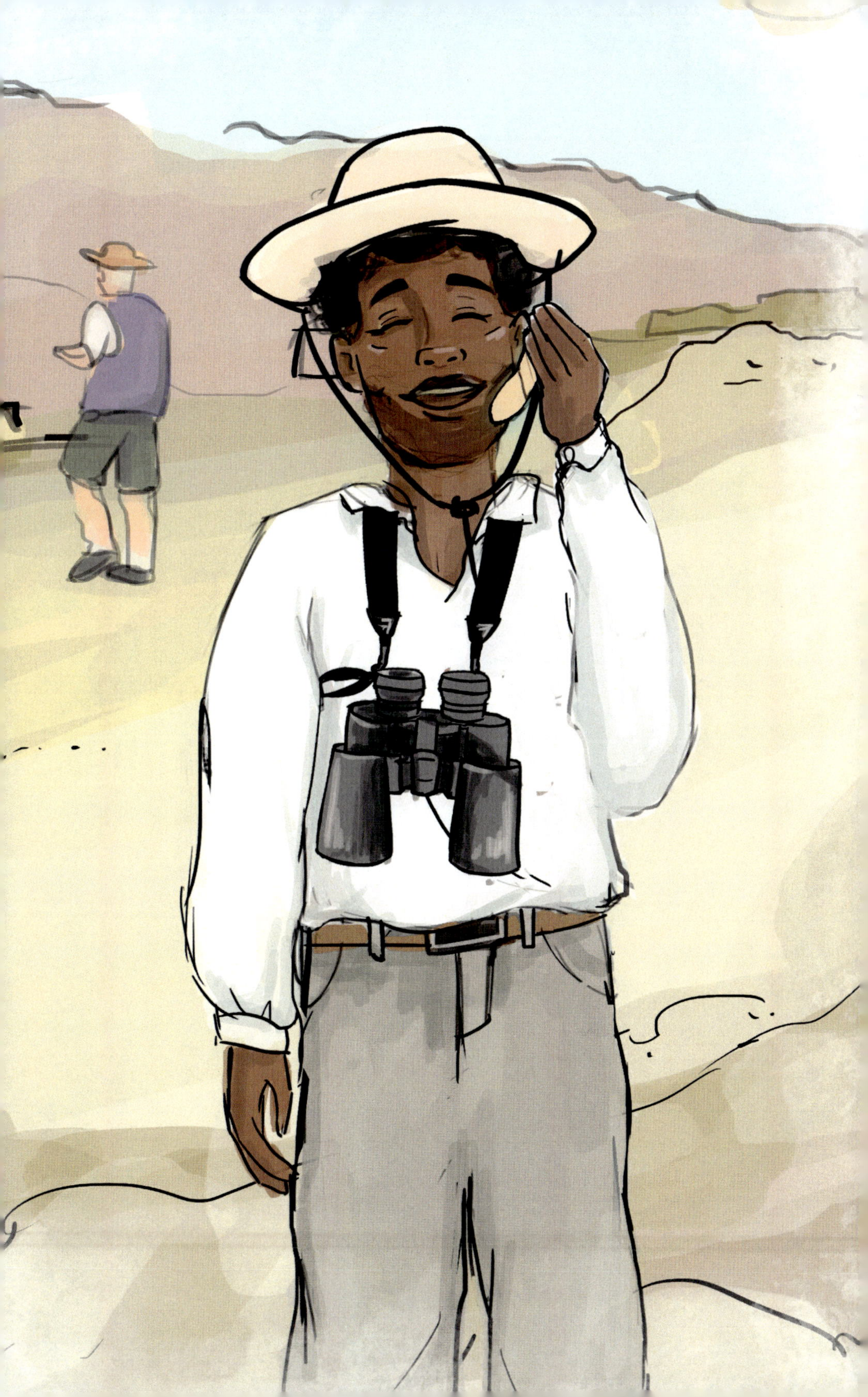

He picks up a stone, and imme diately, it glows, and a large glowing circle appears on the wall. He sees himself in the large glowing circle.

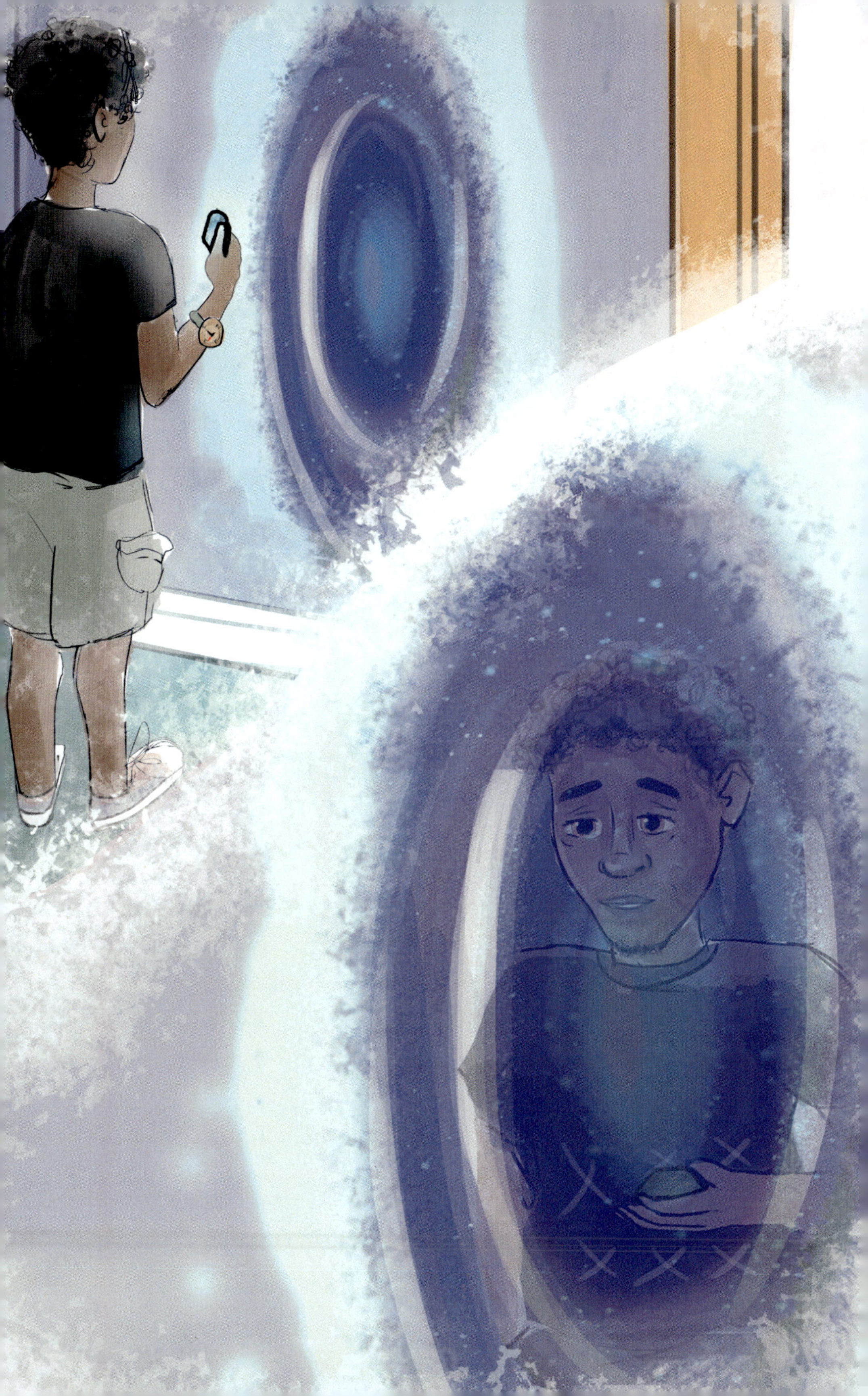

Sebastian drops the stone, and the circle disappears. He walks to the wall and slowly steps back.

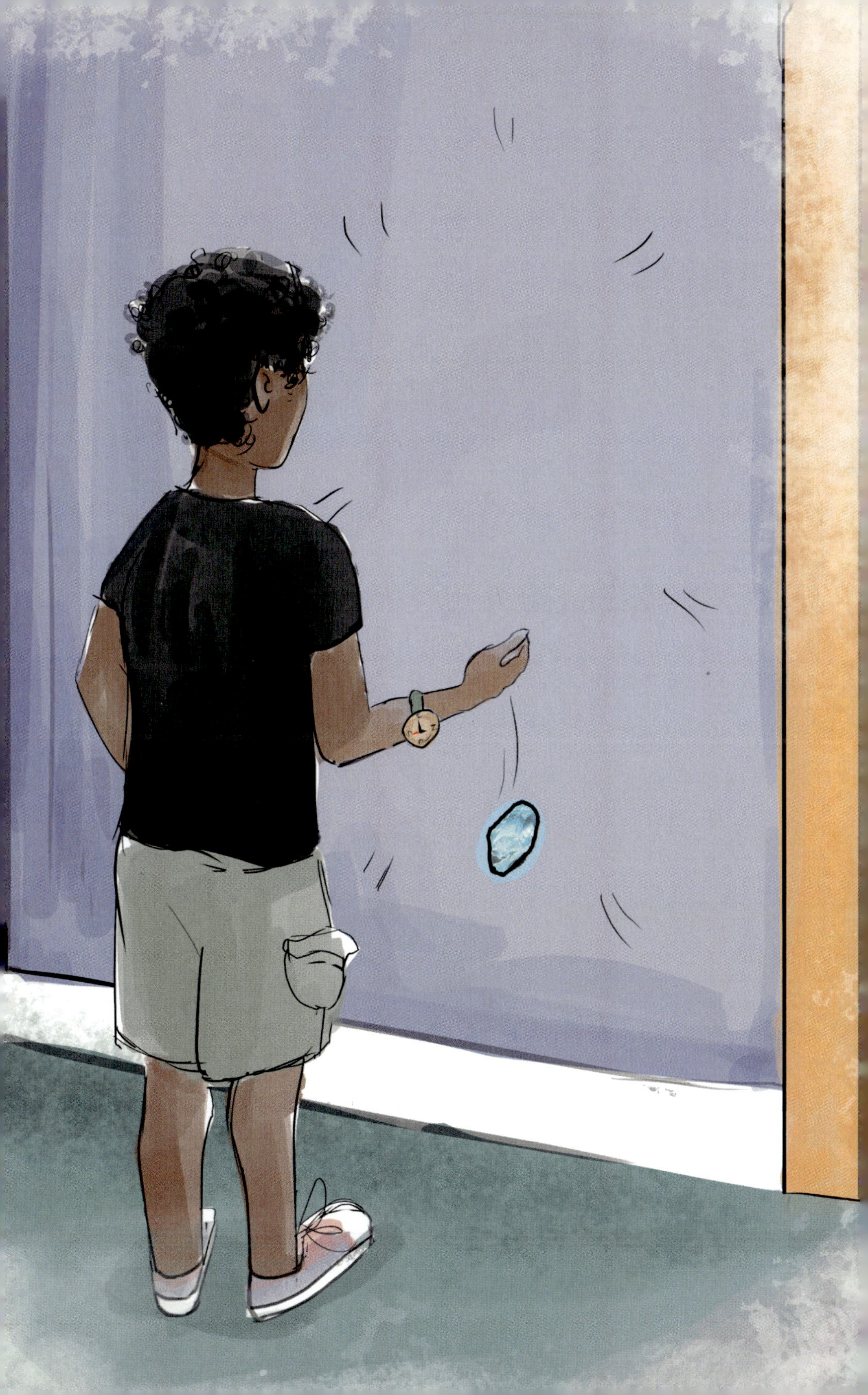

Sebastian picks the stone up again and is thrown into the magical portal.

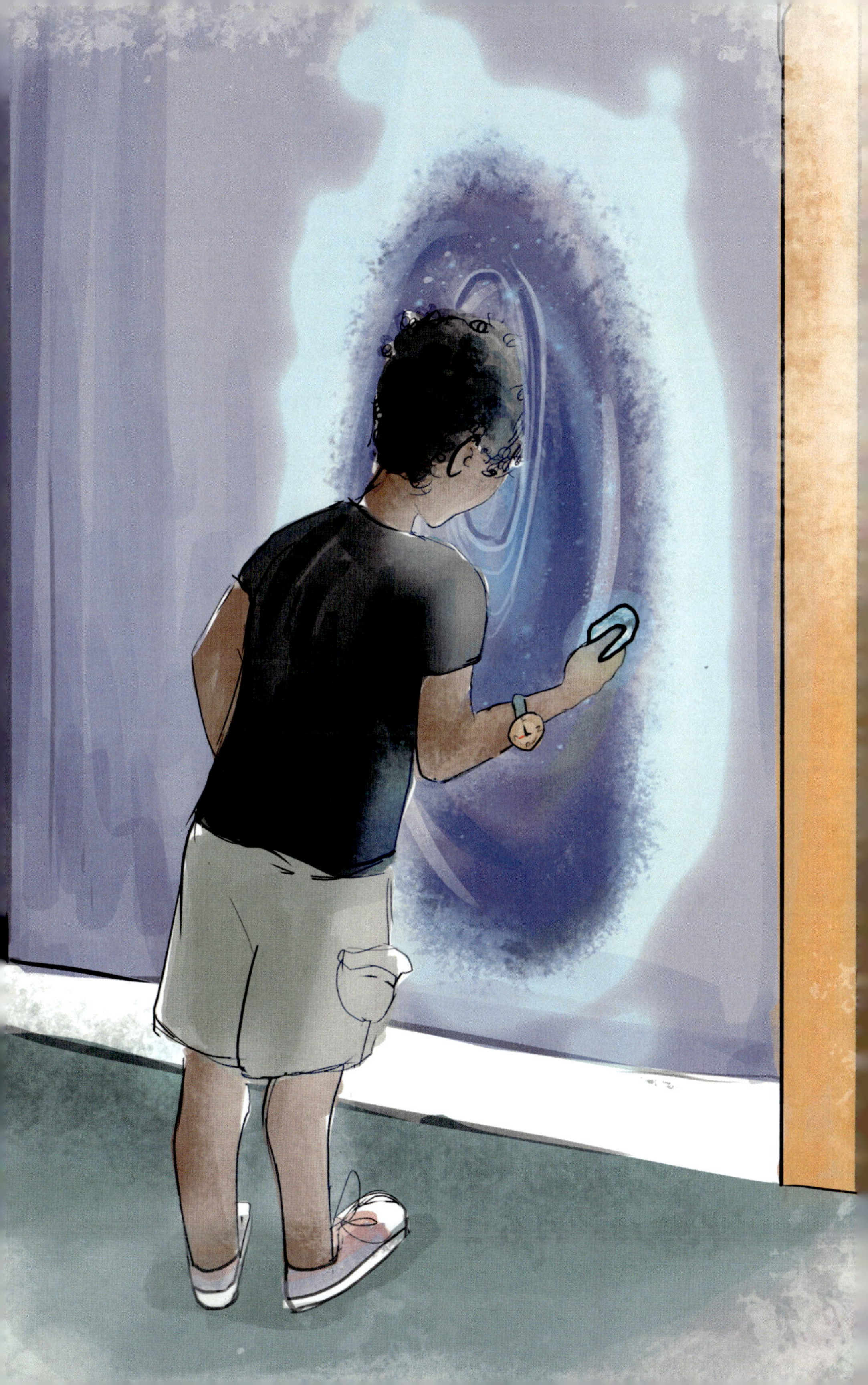

The next morning, he rushes downstairs to tell his mom. His mom tells him to stop it immediately. "Your dad is missing! Stop.

I can't take anything else." Sebastian's head drops, and he walks away.

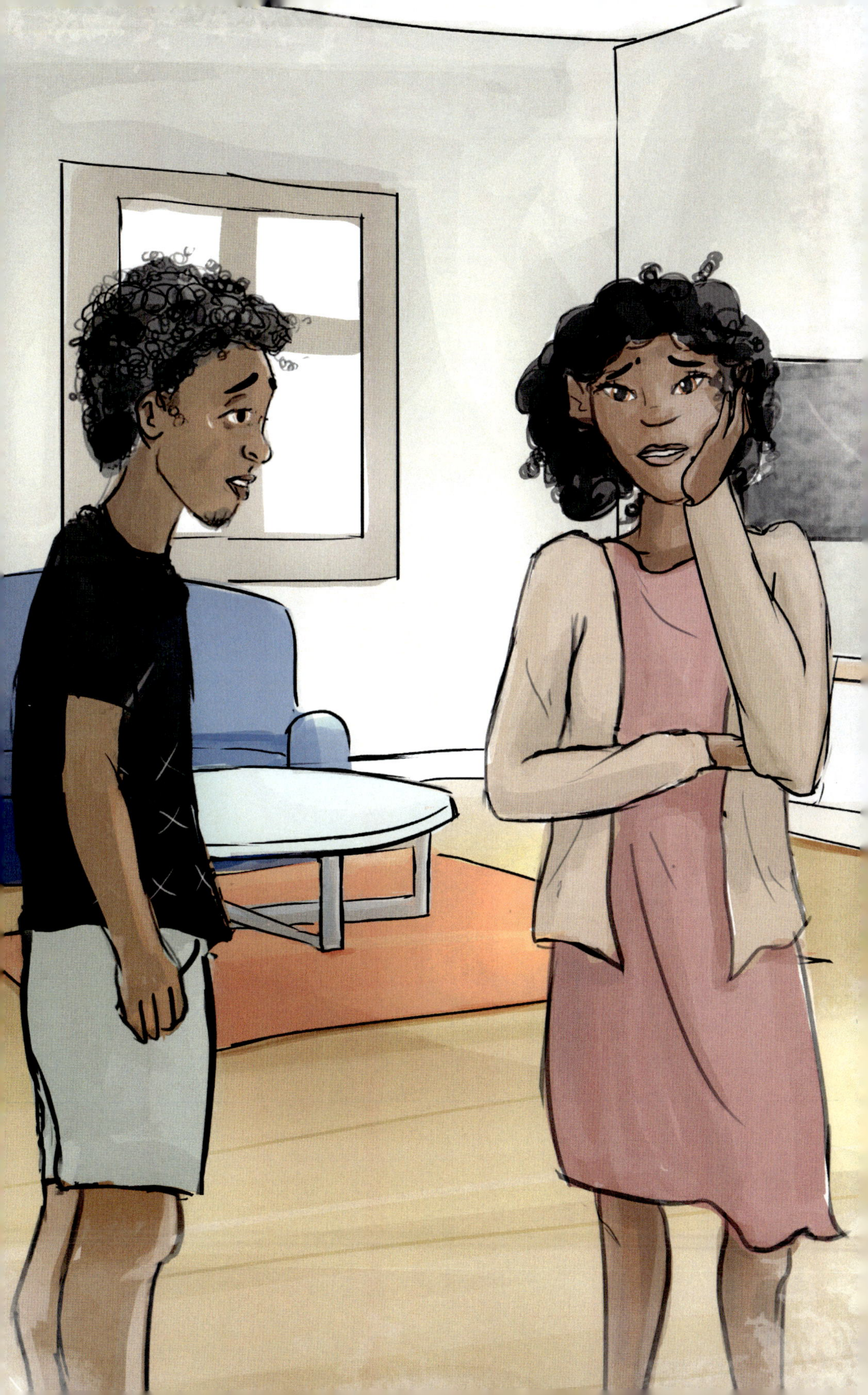

In the other part of the city, Violet, 17, fights with Gina, her aunt. Gina demands her to get in the car. Violet looks back at her home, which was de stroyed by a fire, barely standing surrounded by debris.

Her uncle, Brad, sits behind the wheel of the car. Violet walks slowly and doesn't speak a word.

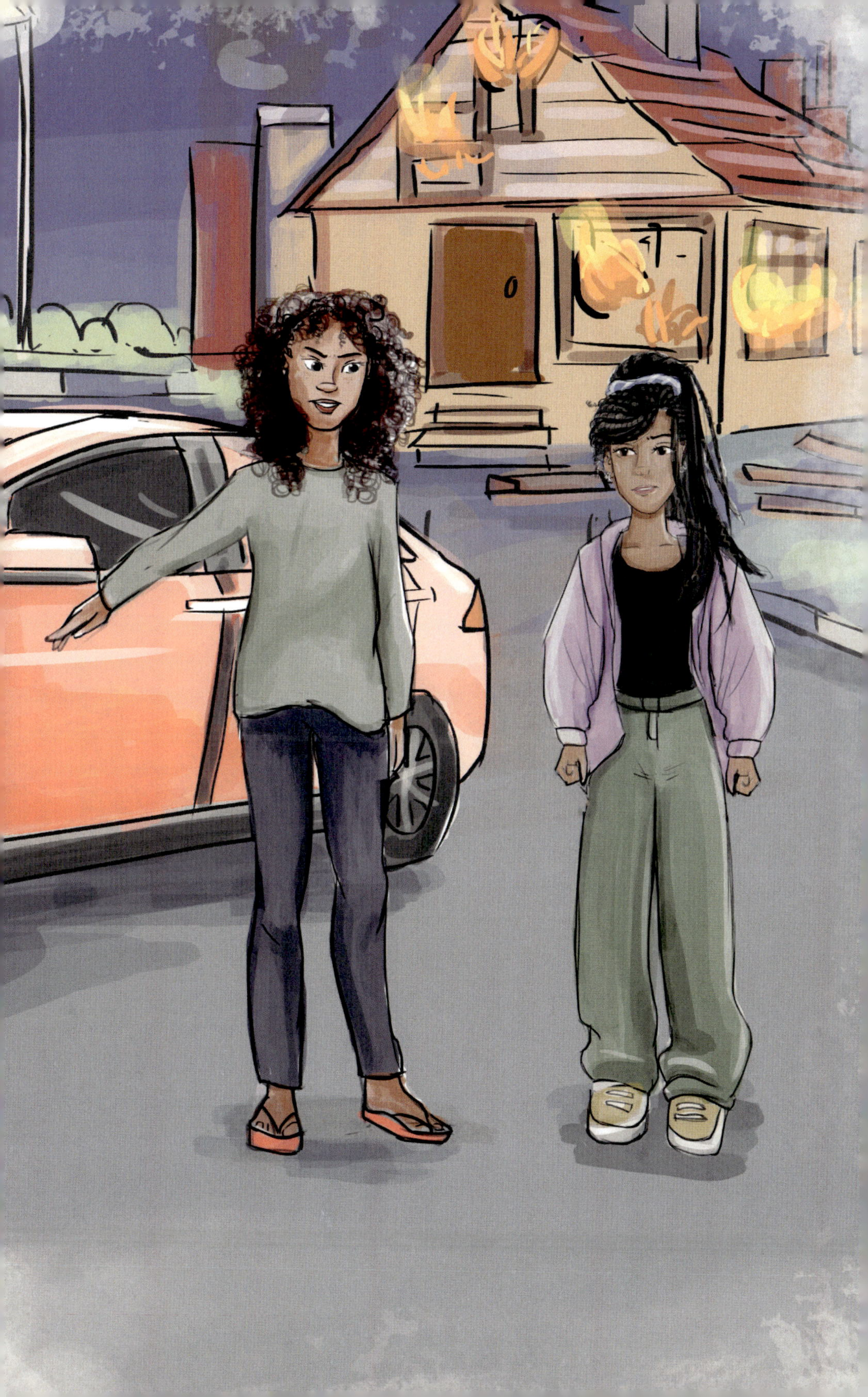

They drive off.

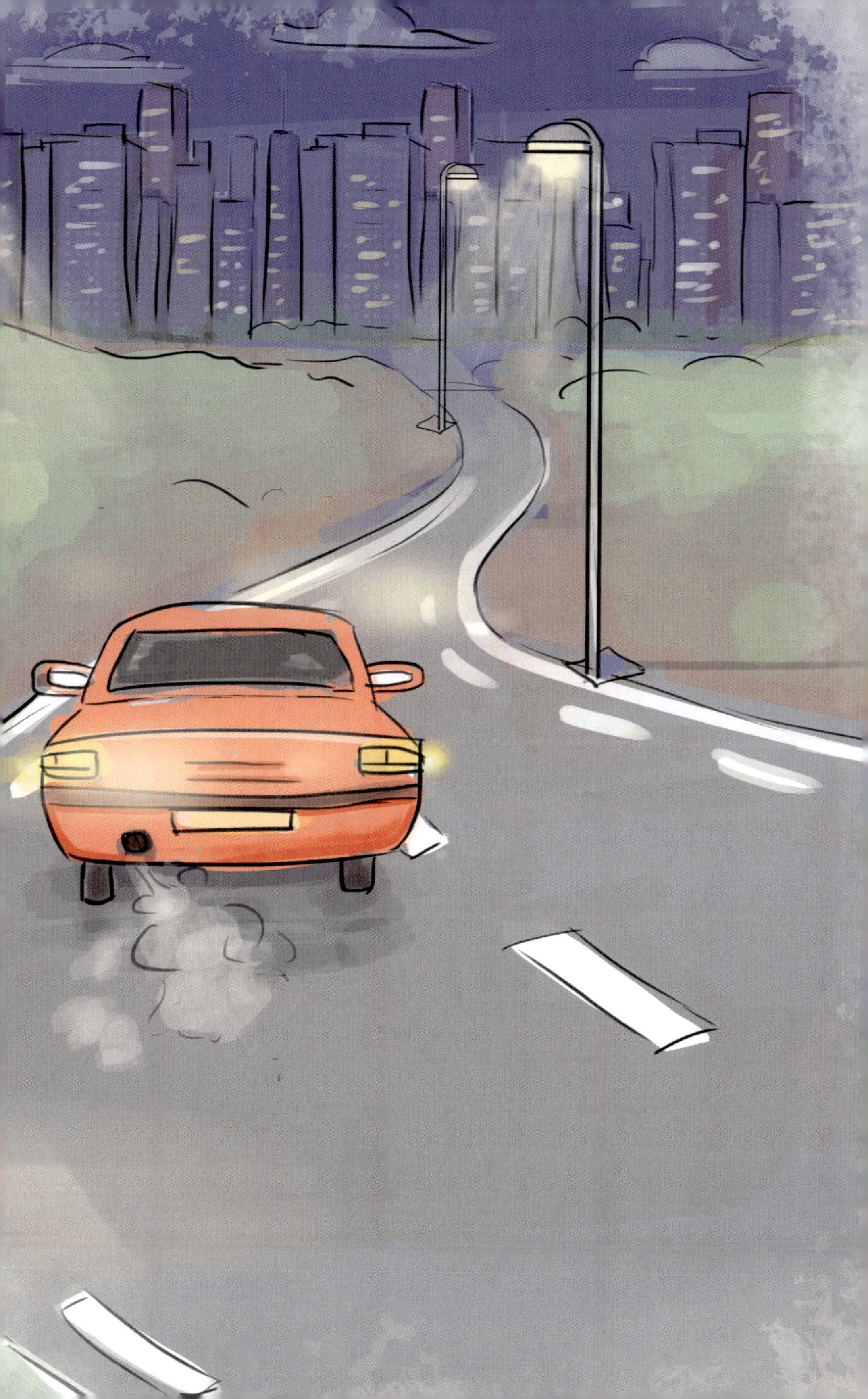

They arrive at home. Violet overhears them talking about her parents. "I blame them, they put this foolishness in her head."

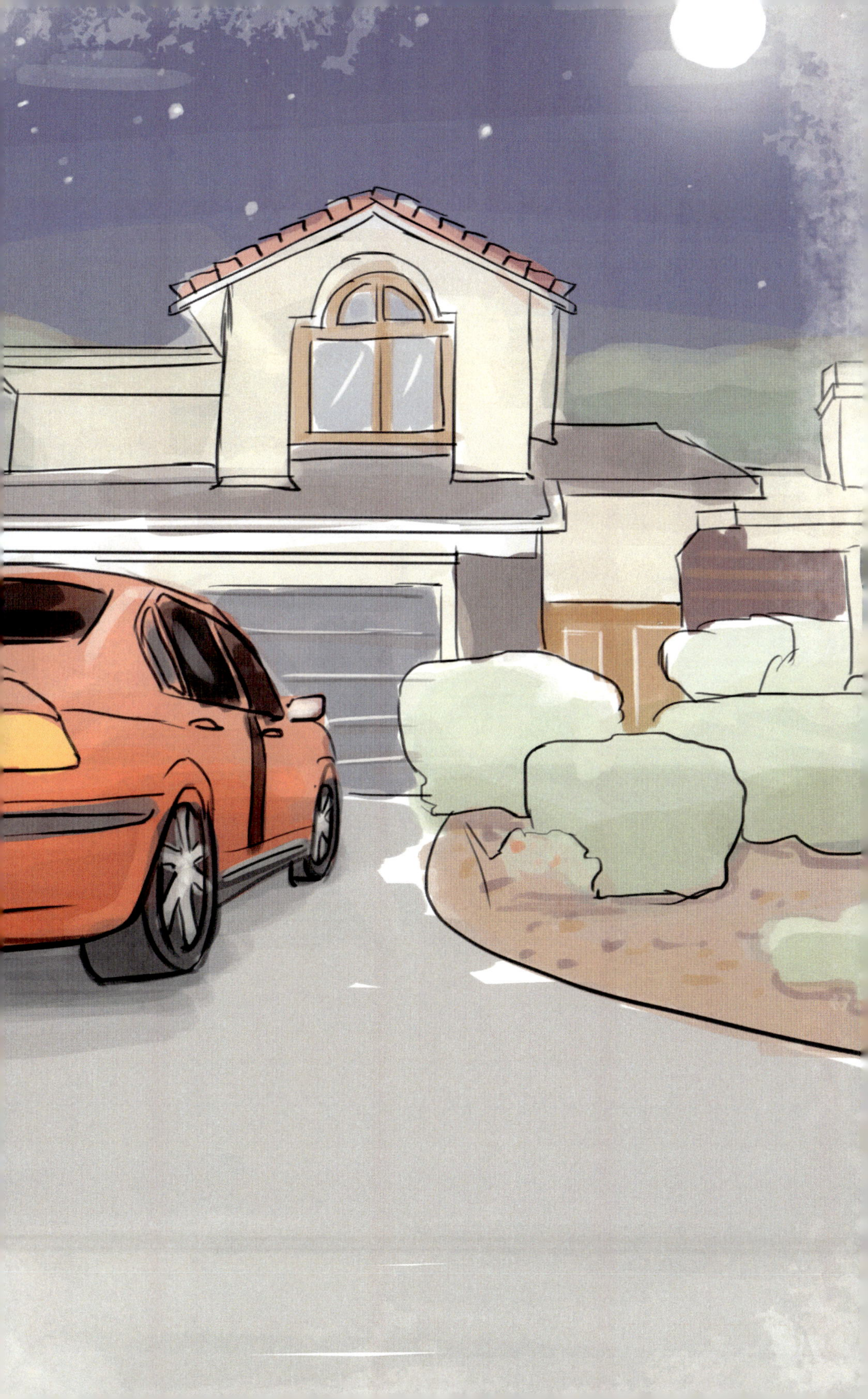

Violet slowly walks back
to her room, upset.

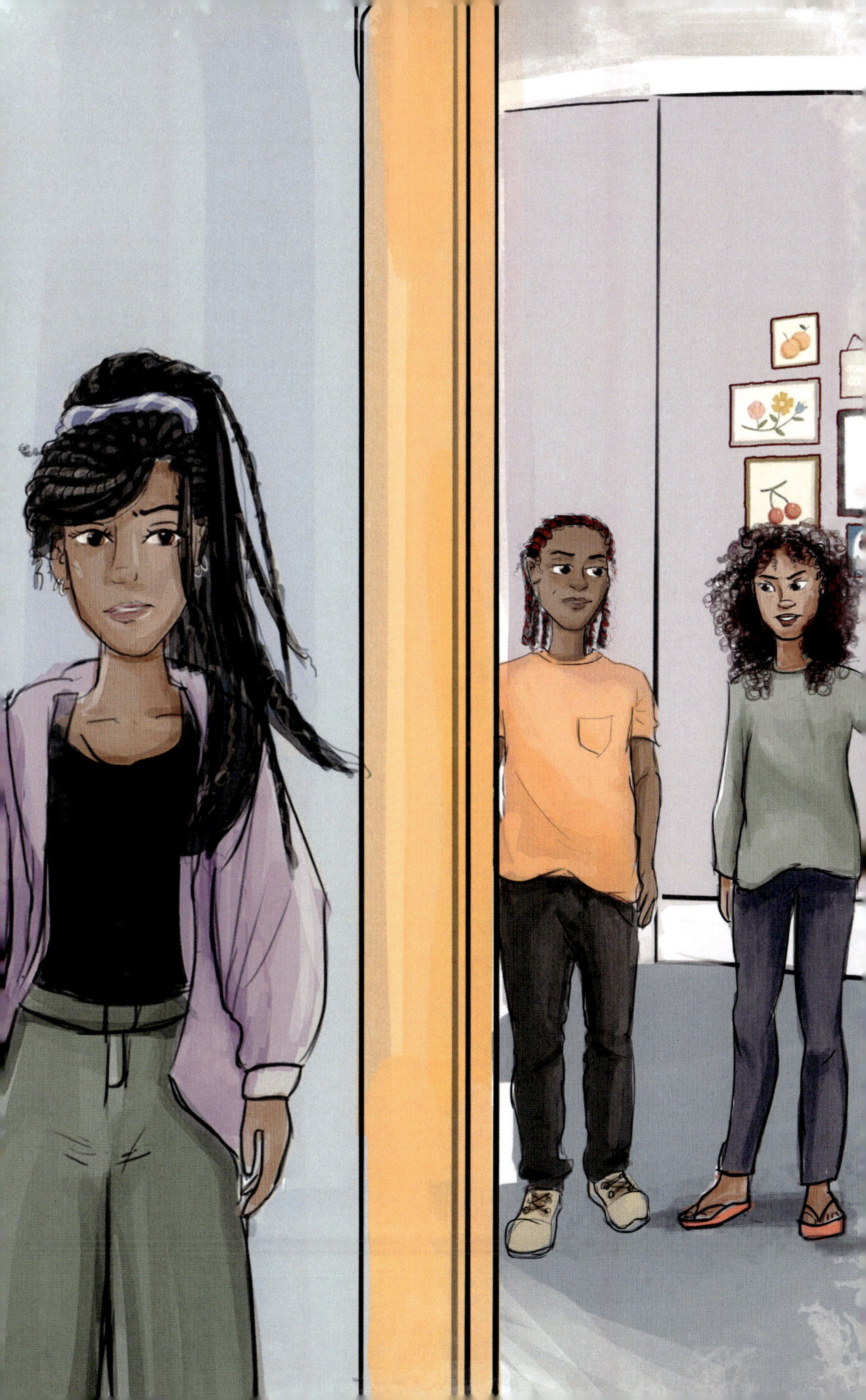

Her aunt Gina calls her down for dinner. At dinner, Violet stares at her plate. Her uncle Brad tells her she has to eat. She doesn't acknowledge him and continues to look down.

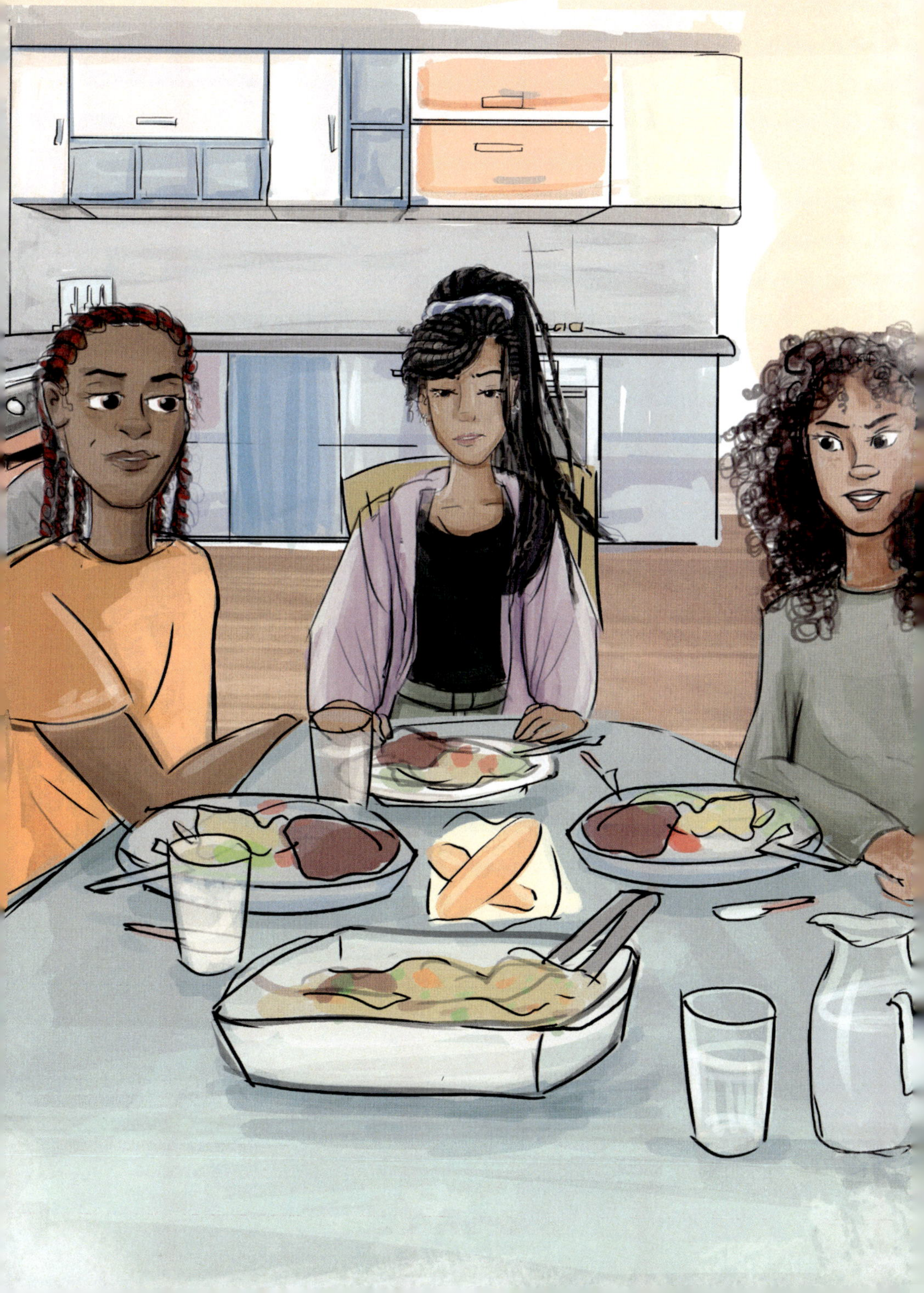

Her aunt becomes upset. "My sister brought this on you. We are trying to provide some normalcy, Violet. "I told her to stop repeatedly! I loved her, but I didn't agree. This is a lot for anyone."

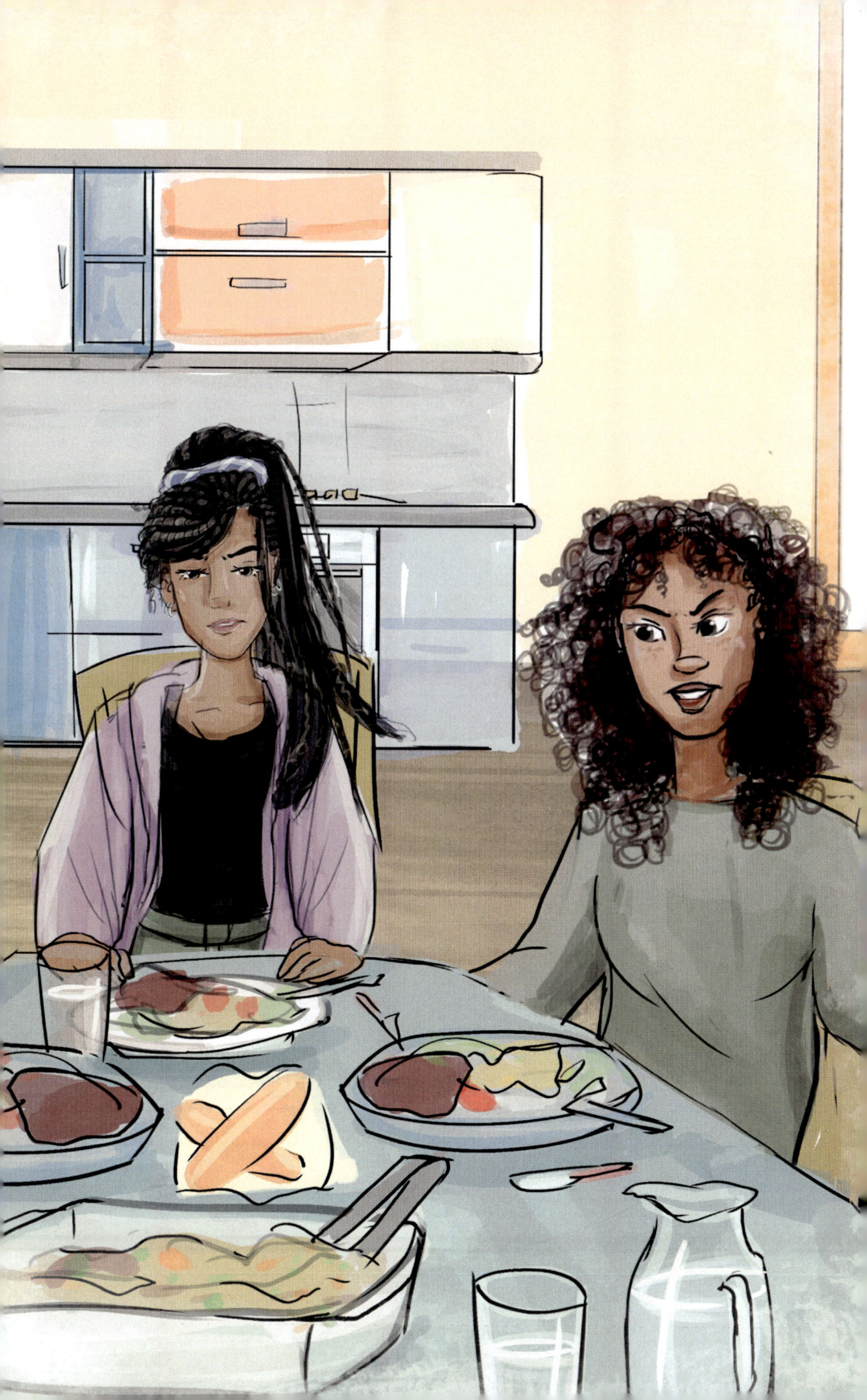

The next morning, they arrive at Dr. Barry's office. Sebastian enters the lobby and sees Violet's aunt throwing her bracelet into the garbage while telling her, "You aren't special!"

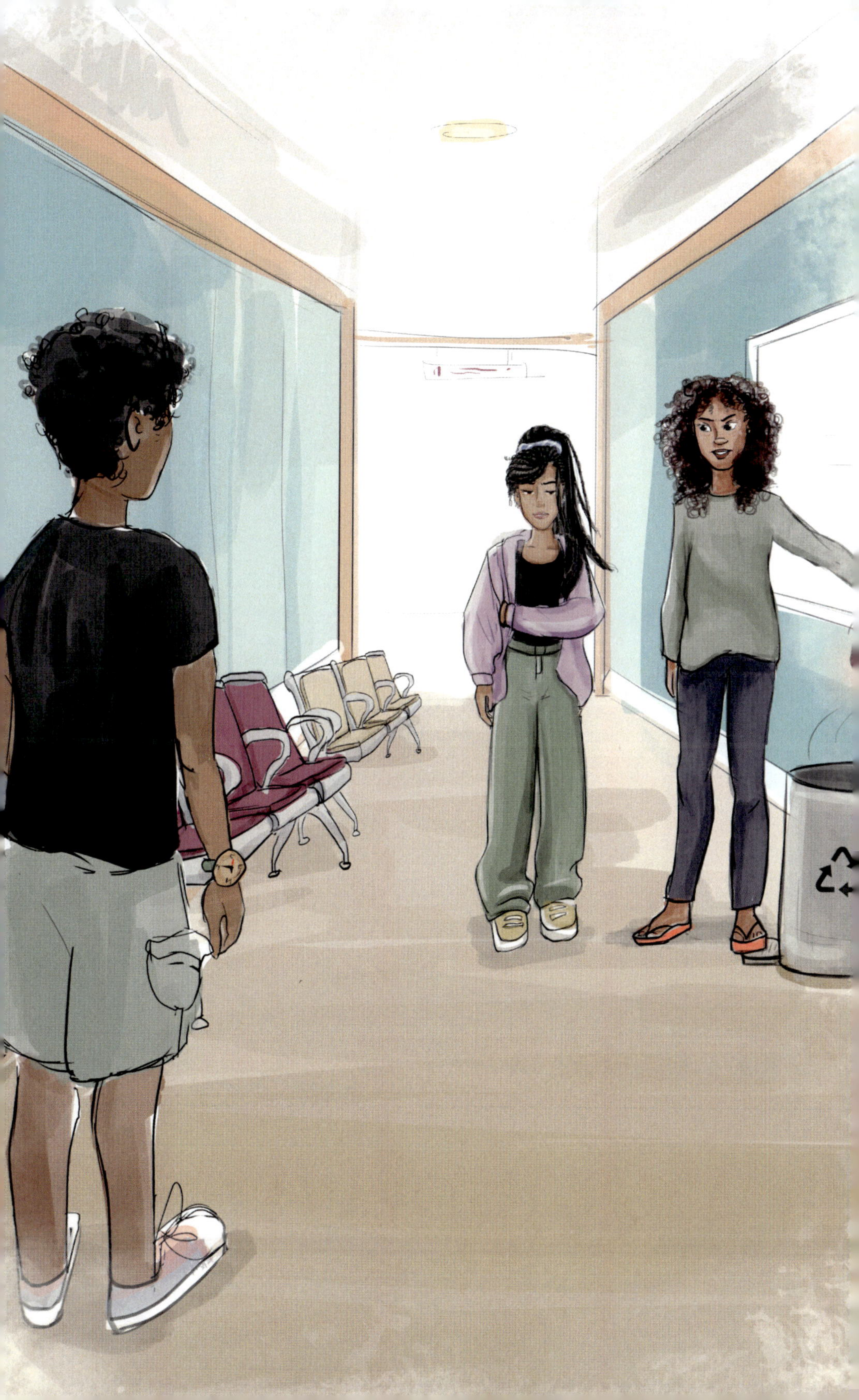

Violet holds back her
emotions. The two head into
the psychiatrist's office.

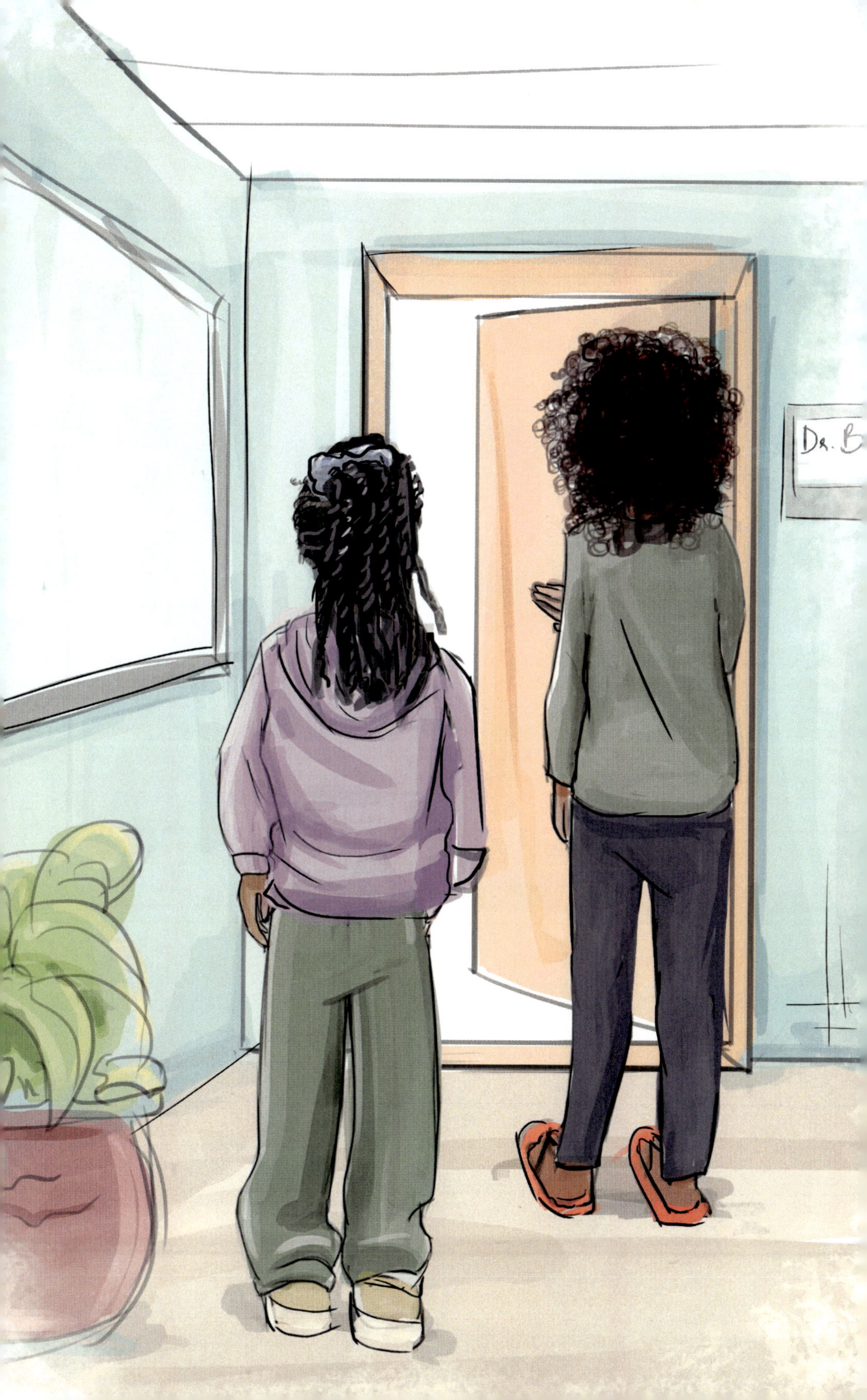
Dr. B

Sebastian's mom is on the phone, trying to call his dad. Violet comes out, and Sebastian hands Violet her bracelet. "You need this. You are special."
They share a smile, and Violet leaves.

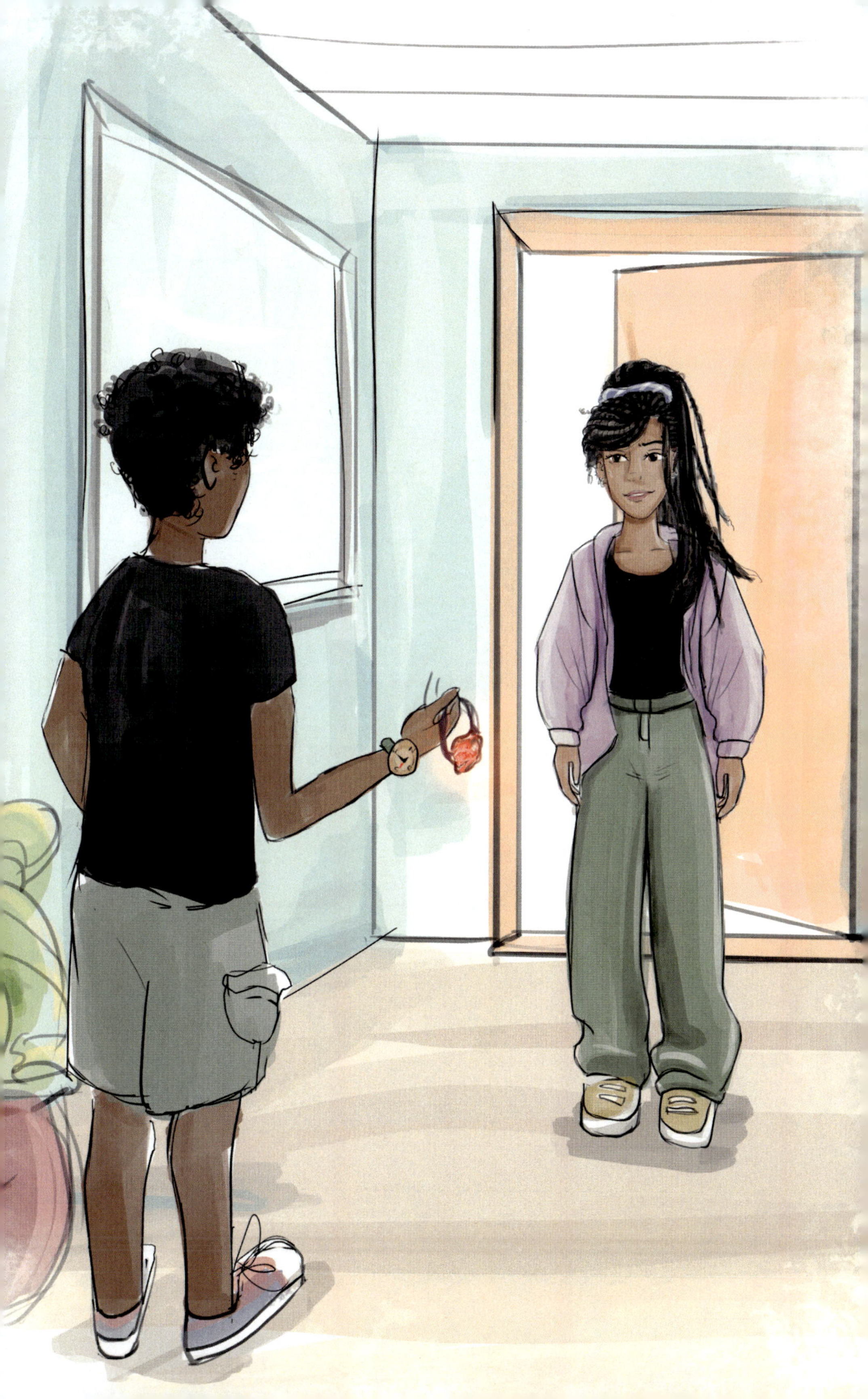

Sebastian enters the office. Brenda Stone sits in the lobby.

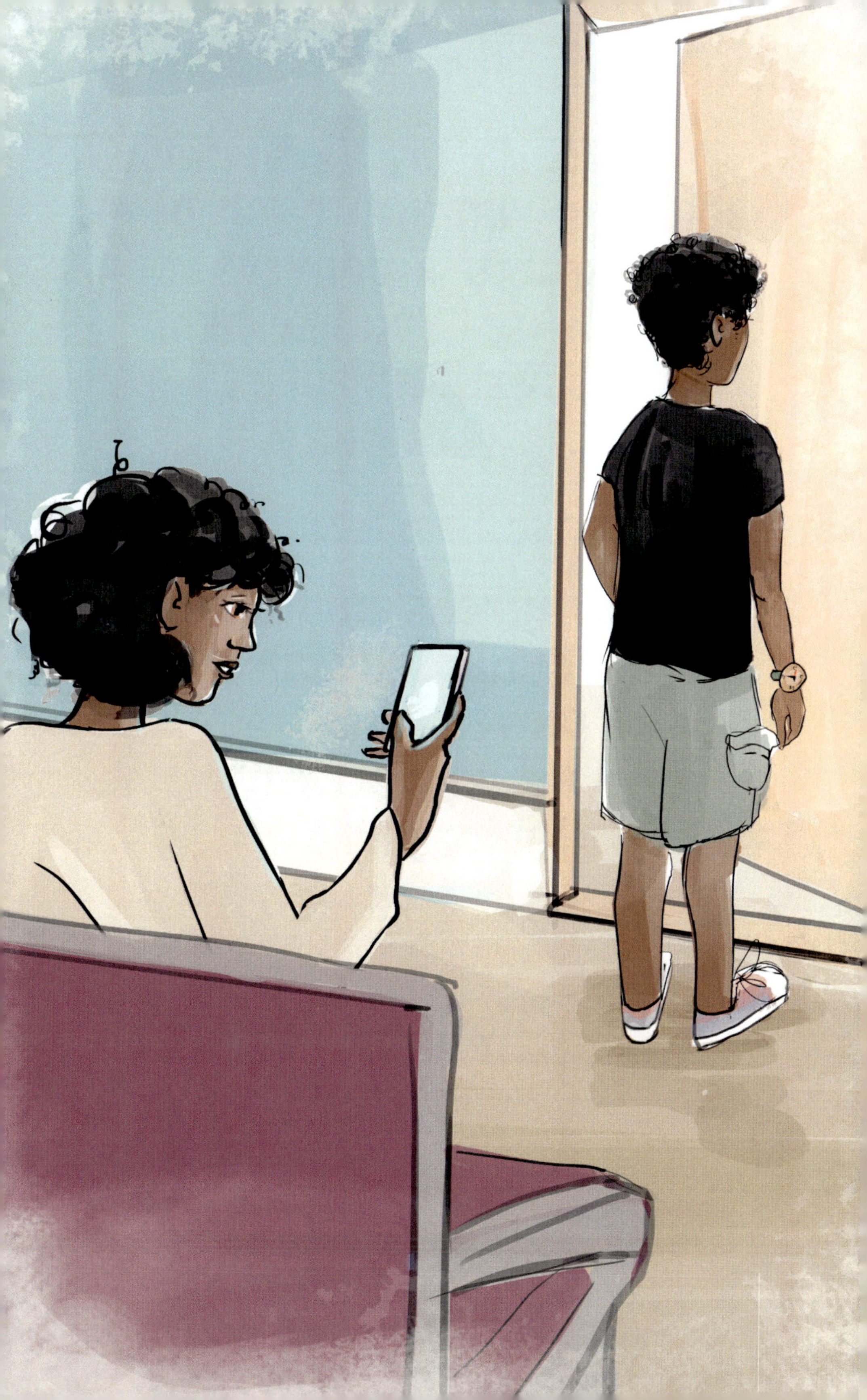

A week later, Violet and Sebastian run into each other. Violet starts a conversation. She asks, "You like him?" Sebastian replies, "He was okay."

Violet agrees and smiles. Sebastian reveals, "I have power, and I believe you do as well." Violet smiles.

Sebastian says, "We are special." The two share a bond. Violet says, "Thanks."

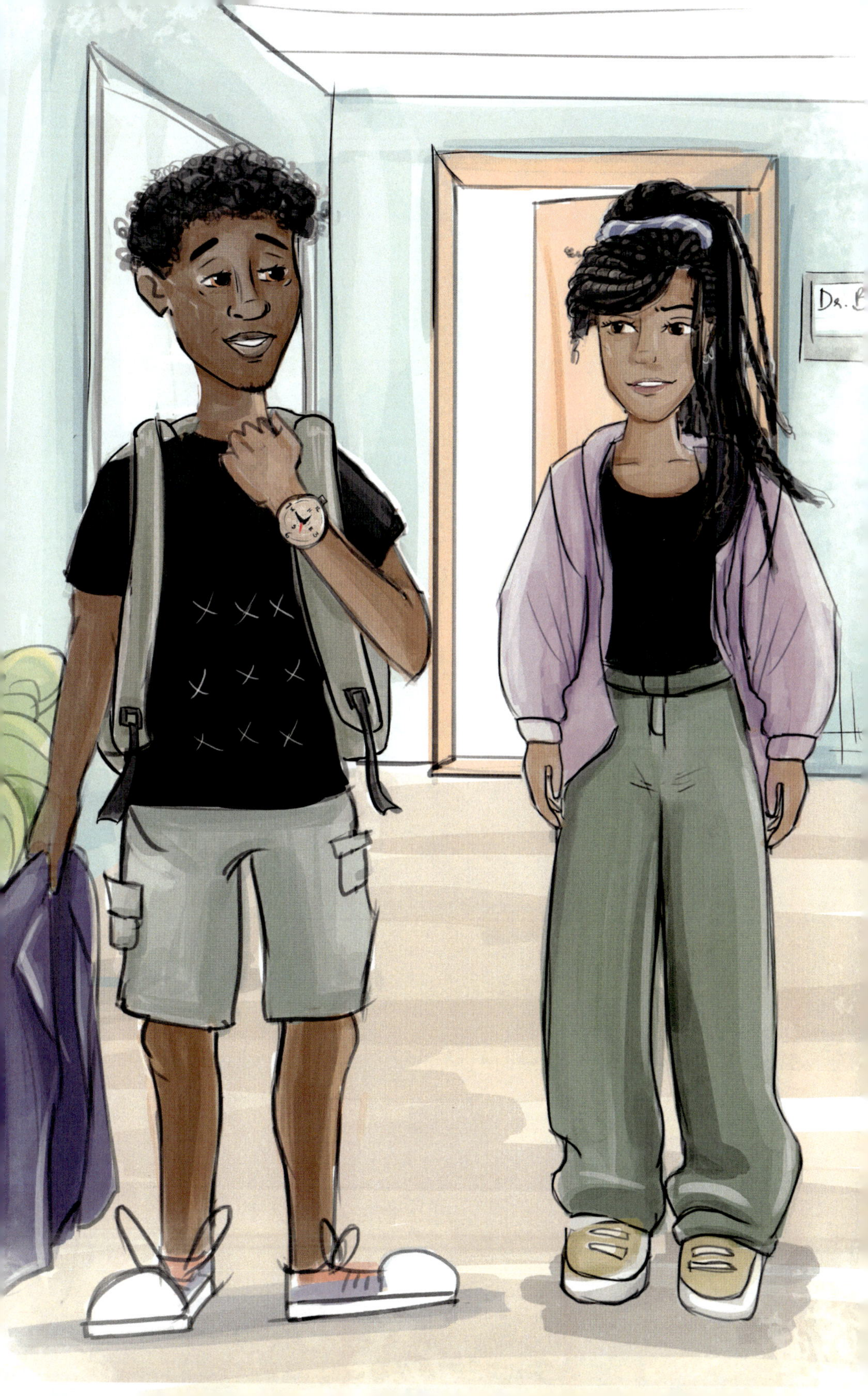
Dr.

The office door opens.
Violet goes inside, and
she looks back and gives
him a big smile.

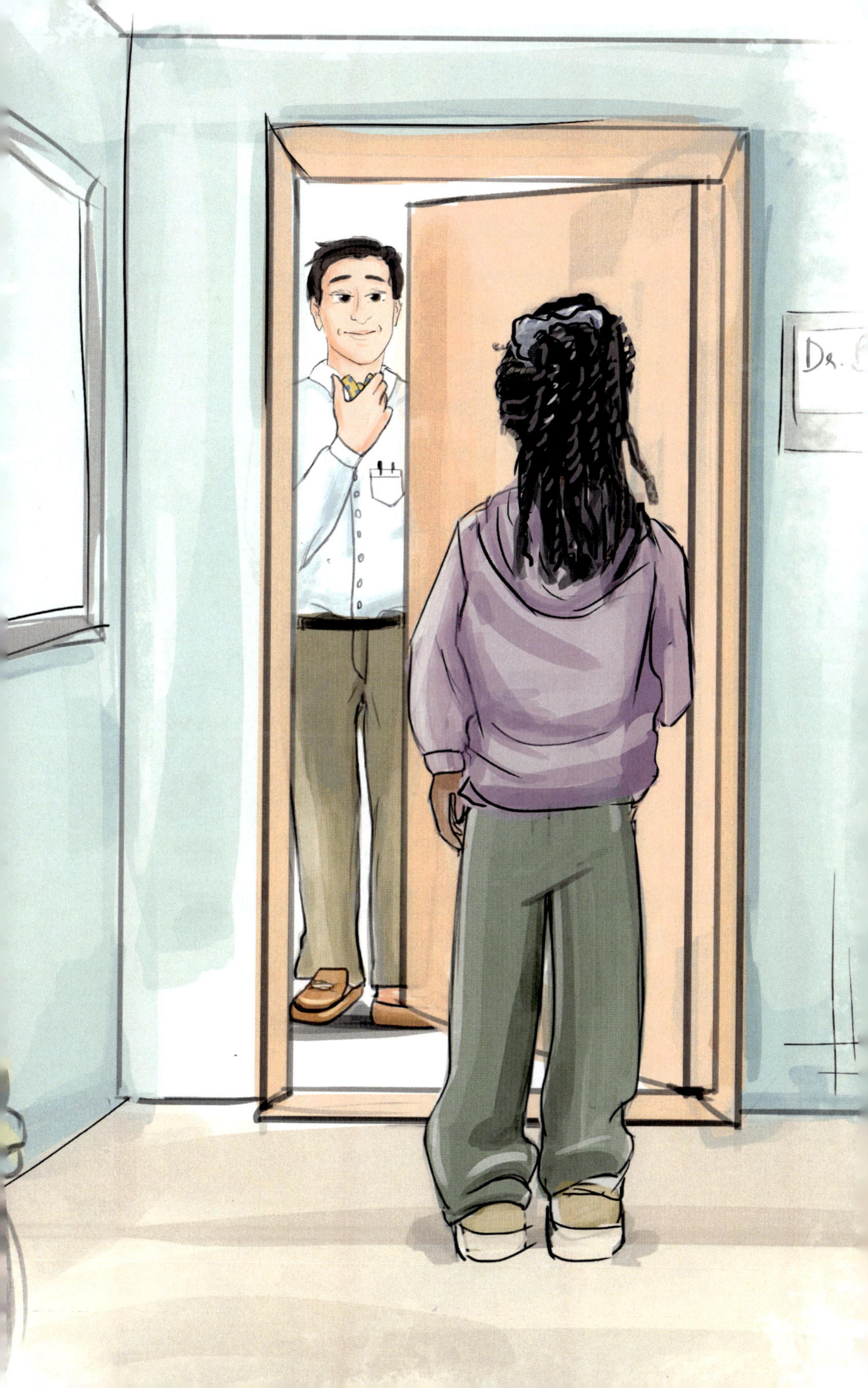
Dr.

A few days later, Sebastian and Violet meet at the library.
Violet asks, "What are you going to do?"
Sebastian says, "I'm going to find my father."
Violet lights up with joy for the first time in months. "I also want answers. Let's go!"

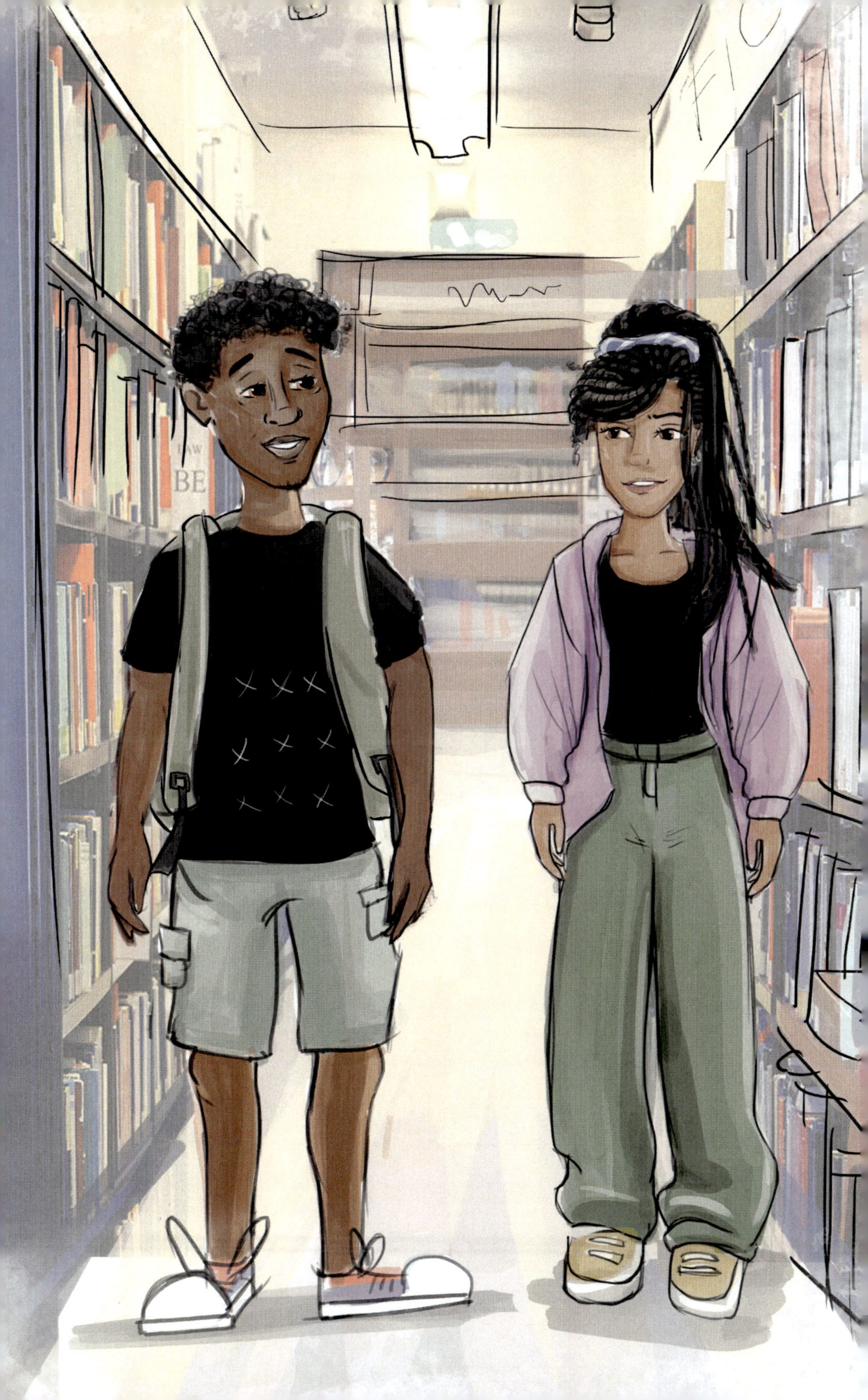

The two are set on a journey of self discovery, hope, and adventure. Sebastian helps her with her new outfit.

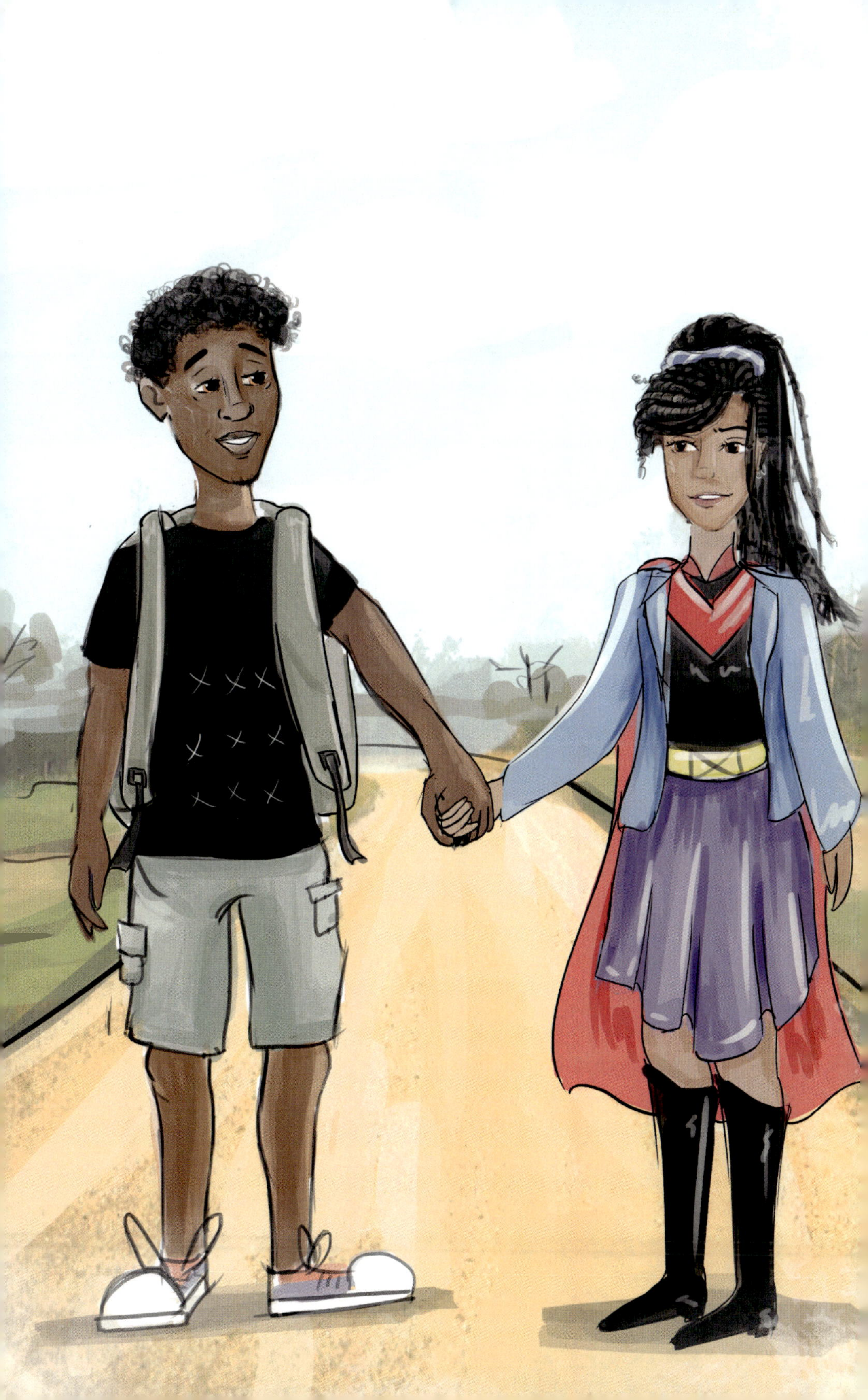

Violet is finally free as she turns into a powerful hurricane. She scoops him up, and they travel down the dirt road. Sebastian is laughing and enjoying the ride.

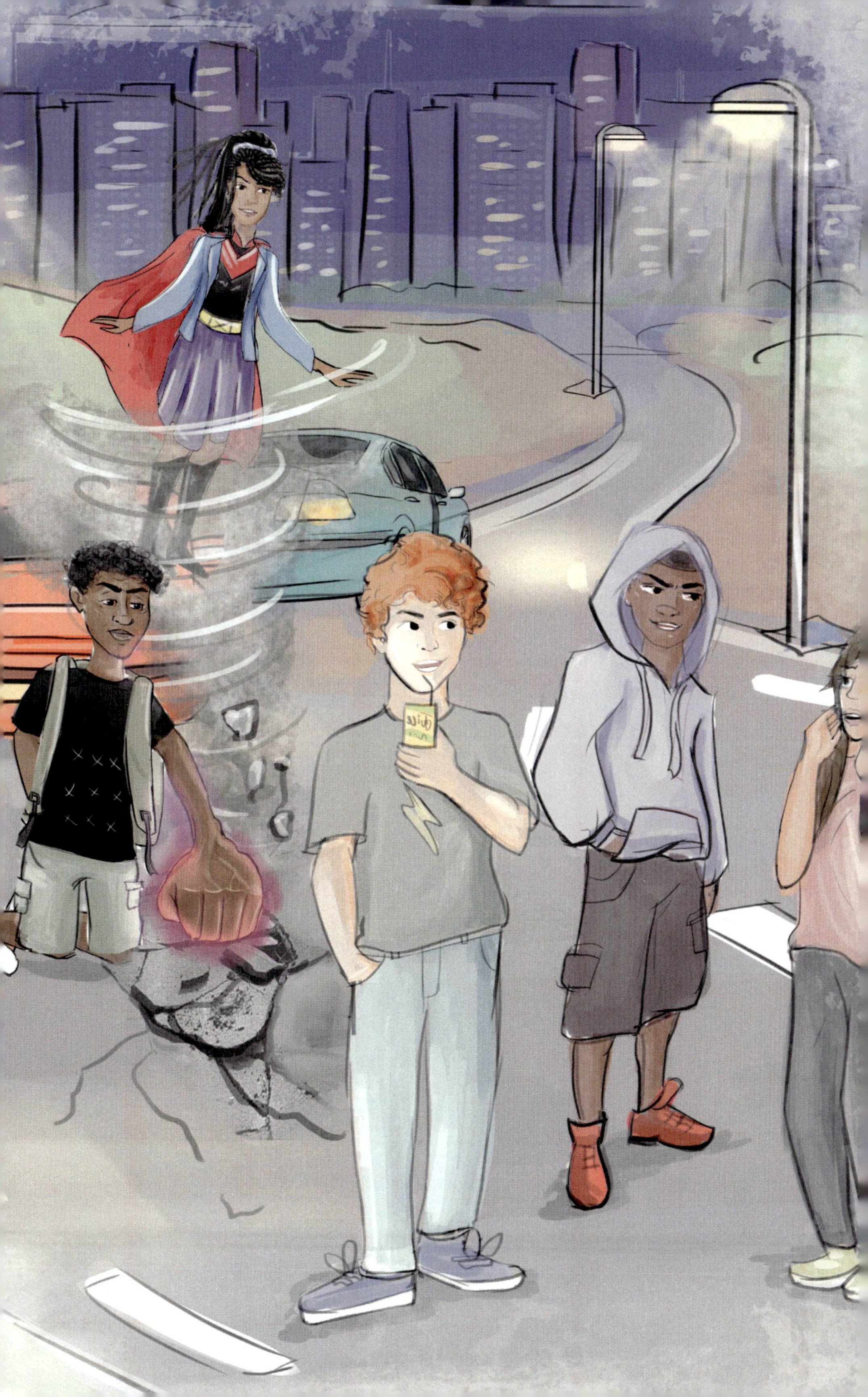

Sebastian's stone glows, and he hears a cry for help. They find a girl in distress. Two boys are torturing the girl. Sebastian's hand becomes large and he hits the cement, cracking it.

He swoops in and picks the girl up. Violet becomes a strong wind, flying the boys into some parked cars. The cars' alarms go off!!!

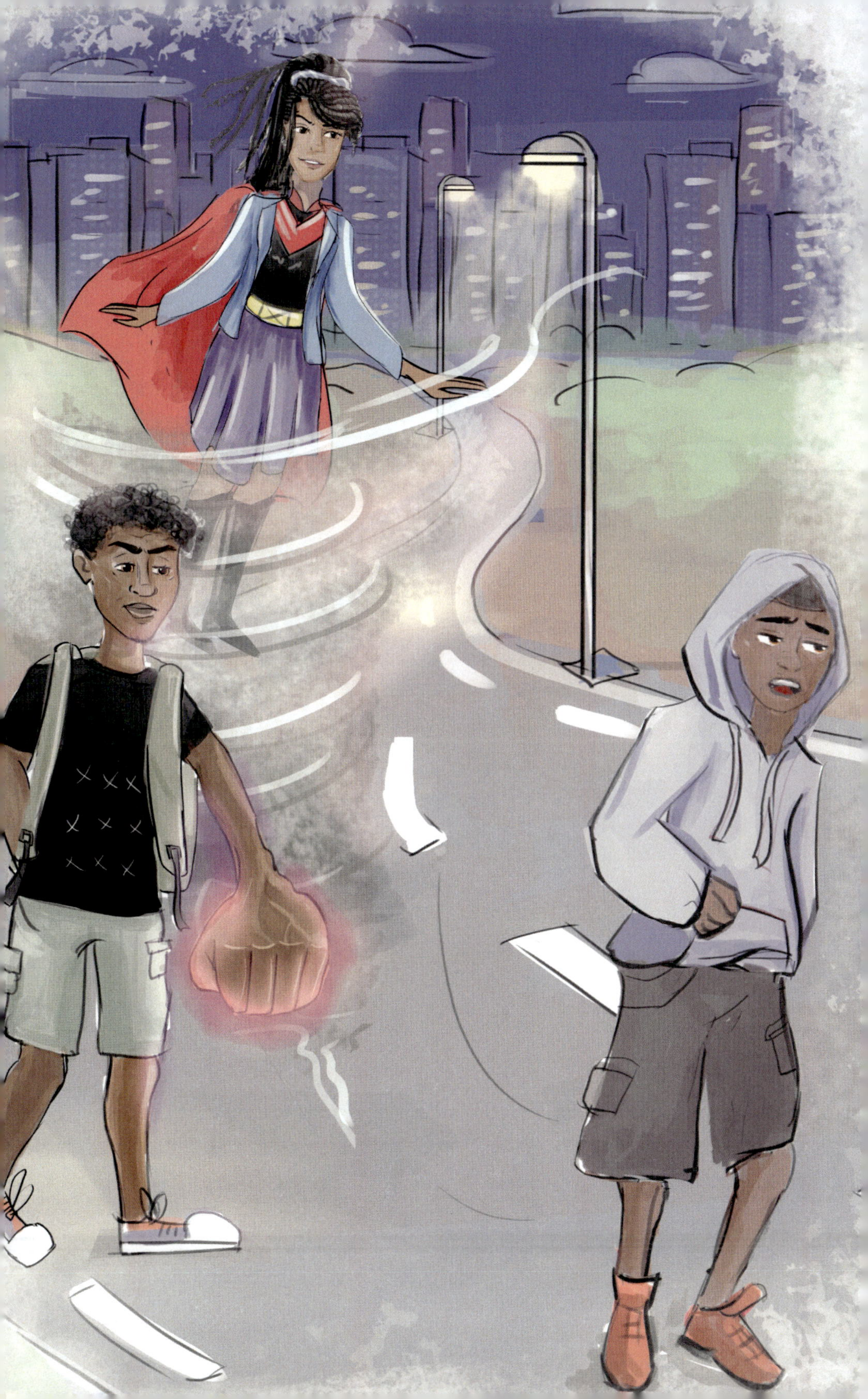

The End

Made in the USA
Middletown, DE
20 October 2024